GHOSTLY TALES AND SINISTER STORIES OF OLD EDINBURGH

Alan J. Wilson

31 October 1991

GHOSTLY TALES & SINISTER STORIES OF OLD EDINBURGH

ALAN J. WILSON, DES BROGAN, FRANK McGRAIL

MAINSTREAM
PUBLISHING

EDINBURGH AND LONDON

First published in Great Britain 1991 by
MAINSTREAM PUBLISHING COMPANY
(EDINBURGH) LTD
7 Albany Street
Edinburgh EH1 3UG

ISBN 1 85158 456 0

A catalogue record for this book is available from the British
Library

Typeset in 11 on 12pt Century School Book by
Falcon Typographic Art Ltd, Edinburgh & London
Printed in Great Britain by Mackays of Chatham, Chatham

CONTENTS

SINISTER STORIES OF OLD EDINBURGH

ACKNOWLEDGMENTS

The authors wish to extend their grateful thanks to the following people without whom this book would probably have remained, like many of our tales, in spirit form only.

Martin R. Harwood for the many hours of thorough and painstaking research and without whom many of the original sources for these tales would never have been discovered; the staff of the Central Library and in particular the Edinburgh Room for their patience, guidance and co-operation; Mr T. D. Wilson who read and re-read the manuscript at each stage of writing; the guides of Mercat Tours, past and present, who retell many of these accounts so vividly in the old dark closes and wynds of Edinburgh; Mr Bill Campbell and the staff of Mainstream Publishing.

The majority of the illustrations are from *Grants Old and New Edinburgh*.

FOREWORD

'If only these buildings could speak,' an old gentleman once said to me, 'what a story they could tell.' How right he was, for Edinburgh's history has been as illustrious and glorious as any city in Europe. But despite the advance of technology as we approach the end of the twentieth century, his hope will always be in vain.

We are fortunate therefore that the history of Edinburgh can still be discovered by reading books such as this. Generals and wars, great political figures and important legislation can be read about elsewhere. This book, equally well researched and written and splendidly illustrated, tells us of the everyday lives — and frequently rather gruesome deaths — of ordinary men and women.

The study of the past should be colourful, adventurous, fascinating and informative. All of these prerequisites have been admirably met. It is difficult to use the word enjoyable when reading of an Edinburgh citizen being cruelly tortured to death or burned at the stake, but as long as we remember and are grateful that such horrors are firmly stuck in the past, we can be amused at and amazed by what our ancestors got up to in the name of justice, morality, religion and science.

It is said that there are five million Scots living within our shores and a further forty million living in various parts of the world. For all those and the many others who come to visit and appreciate our city, this book can only enrich and enhance their stay in the capital. I feel it will be a welcome addition to the shelves of our bookshops and to the bookshelves of our homes, wherever in the world they may be.

The Rt. Hon. Eleanor McLaughlin
Lord Provost

GHOSTLY TALES
OF
HISTORIC EDINBURGH

BURNING PASSION

Almost seven centuries ago the lands of Gilmerton and Liberton, on the outskirts of the city, were owned by the gallant knight, Sir John Herring. Sir John and his great friend, Sir Alexander Ramsay of Dalhousie, were famous in their day for their wild and constant personal raids into England.

Sir John had two lovely daughters, Margaret and Giles. The baronet had intended that his petite, demure daughter Margaret should marry his brother's son, Patrick. He would then make them heirs to the greater part of the estate. But although Margaret was beautiful, she was moody, melancholy and prone to extreme fits of depression. She was a keen churchgoer and strictly followed all the rites and observances

Gilmerton

of her religion. Each day she would make a rough cross-country journey to Newbattle Abbey to be taught by a handsome young monk.

They studied and discussed the Gospels and Scriptures but as time passed the monk's eyes veered from the pages of the ancient religious tomes to the beauty of his pupil's face. The resulting motions were not one-sided. In spite of the sacred laws which forbade a man of God to have such feelings for a woman, Margaret became his mistress. At the abbey they discussed ways and means of meeting secretly. To do so in the abbey was out of the question. The abbot was strict and would punish the flouting of such rigid laws without mercy. At last the monk remembered a little farm in Gilmerton called 'The Grange'. It was secluded, surrounded by trees and ideal as a clandestine meeting place. By coincidence, the lovely young widow who owned it was also having an affair with another monk at Newbattle.

Secret though the meetings were, neighbours' suspicions were soon aroused and tongues began to wag. The hooded Margaret was frequently seen hurrying across the dark path to the farmstead. The gossip soon reached Sir John. Raging, he summoned his daughter. If ever she returned to 'The Grange', he threatened he would kill her instantly. The farm was out of bounds and she must not see the monk again. She accepted her father's demands.

Beside herself with fear caused by her father's fierce words, the distraught Margaret paced up and down in her room, impatiently waiting for darkness to fall. Despite her promise, the monk had to be warned and, after all, it would be their last meeting.

Some hours later, Sir John called once again for his daughter. But her room was empty. Ringing for the servants he ordered them to search for her. She had to be found. With lit torches they searched the house, the flames casting weird shadows in the gloomy corners of the old mansion. But Margaret had vanished.

Sir John knew where she was. Ordering new torches and two servants, Sir John, followed by the men, headed off to 'The Grange'. Across the fields they went, stumbling over the rough pasture and the drainage ditches. 'The Grange' was in complete darkness. The religious house was locked and barred. The only sound was the heavy breathing of the knight and his servants.

Ever more enraged he called for his daughter. He rushed at the door, battering it wildly with his fists. But there was no response. The couple were in there. This he knew. But they lay cringing in horror, too terrified to move or to open up to the rampaging knight. They must have heard his order to the servants to gather up dried brushwood and pile it up around the house.

This done, Sir John seized the two torches and deliberately set fire to the thatched roof and the gathered fuel. In seconds the whole house was ablaze. No one could get near it. No one could get out. The poor incinerated lovers died — burned to death in each other's arms.

Horror-stricken by his deed Sir John raced away from the scene, his lovely daughter left as a charred corpse in the ashes of the farmhouse. Arriving in great haste at the mansion he packed a leather bag and fled to the coast where he boarded a ship.

News of the event reached the king who immediately confiscated Sir John's entire estates. But Sir John's great friend Sir Walter Somerville of Carnwath did his best to help him. He pointed out to the king and to the Abbot of Newbattle how scandalous the lives of the two monks had been.

Soon afterwards, Sir John with his other lovely daughter, Giles, returned secretly to Scotland. They hid at Sir Walter's castle. He begged Sir Walter to intervene with the king.

But in the castle, coming into constant contact with the lovely Giles, the result was inevitable. Sir Walter fell in love. Once again Sir John displayed his displeasure — but the initiative was with Sir Walter. Using Giles as a lever, he bargained with Sir John that if he could obtain the king's pardon he could have her — and 'half the lands of Gilmerton should be settled on him and his wife and hiers . . . irredeemable for ever.'

After much argument the king agreed and Sir Walter got all he wanted.

'The Grange' was rebuilt but the new enlarged building never used its former name. Today it is the Melville Grange

Farm and it is said that only very recently in the corridor of the farmhouse the wife of the owner saw a ghost! A young woman dressed in white. Could this be the spirit of the lovely Margaret still haunting the scene of her horrific death after more than 700 years?

THE BAPHOMET

The Knights Templar have always been a curious bunch of military churchmen. Thrown out of many countries, they made their headquarters for a time in Edinburgh. The house in which they were based still stands.

In 1309, however, two of their order were on trial in Edinburgh. The charge against them was levied by the clergy of Holyrood Abbey. They were accused of adorning the image of a horned head in their 'temple' in the Canongate. In similar trials in other lands this effigy was alluded to as 'the Baphomet' or the Sabbatic goat.

The Knights Templar were very lucky. Instead of being burned at the stake for devil worship they were simply dispossessed of their lands which lay between St Leonards and the southern corner of Holyrood Park. Had their adoration of the diabolical fiend taken place in France, they should have undoubtedly been dispossessed of their lives as well.

THE KING OF TRAITORS

In the reign of King James I, some five centuries ago, Walter, Earl of Atholl had been told by a group of witches that he would soon be crowned king of Scotland. Believing this wholeheartedly and blinded by ambition, the earl entered into a horrid conspiracy with his grandson, Robert Graham. It was decided that with the assistance of some execrable villains the two men would kill the king. And so it was that while visiting the Dominican monastery near Perth, the band of villains broke into the religious house and assassinated His Majesty.

Far from being proclaimed king, the earl was arrested as the principal instigator of the murder. His punishment in Edinburgh was prolonged for three days.

On the first day he was placed upon a cart, on which a kind of crane, in the form of a stork, was erected. The ropes of the crane tied round his ankles, he was drawn up by pulleys and then suddenly let fall to the ground, by which he suffered the most excruciating pain from the dislocation of his joints.

On the second day he was elevated upon a pillory and crowned with a red-hot iron which bore the inscription 'The King of Traitors'. He was then placed upon a hurdle, and drawn at a horse's tail through the High Street of Edinburgh.

On the third day he was stretched out on a platform and, while he was still alive, his intestines and heart were taken out and thrown onto a fire. He was then decapitated and his head was fixed upon a long pole and publicly displayed. Finally his body was quartered with three of the quarters being sent to Perth, Stirling and Aberdeen.

But what of the grandson, Robert? After all it was he who had actually assassinated the king. The royal blood had been drawn by his own hands.

As punishment he was carried through the city on a cart with his right hand nailed to the gallows erected in the vehicle. Throughout the journey the executioner thrust red-hot iron spikes into his thighs, shoulders and limbs and, on occasion, a very short distance from his vital parts.

His life, like that of his grandfather was terminated by being beheaded and quartered.

THE PUNISHMENT OF BEGGARS

In the reign of James I no one between 14 and 70 years of age was allowed to beg unless he or she was unable to work. If able-bodied persons were found begging in the streets they would be burned on the cheek and banished.

In the reign of James IV no one was allowed to beg, 'except cruiked-folk, seik-folk, impotent-folk and weak-folk, under pain of a merk.' Parliament also stated that any who pretended to be 'fools' would be arrested, clapped in irons or nailed by their ears to the Tron and thereafter their ears would be cut off and they would be banished from the country. If they returned and were caught again they would be hanged.

In the reign of James VI strange and idle beggars were put in the stocks or irons, scourged and burnt through the ears with hot irons, unless 'an honest and respectable man' came forward and offered to take them into his service. If, however, they deserted and were caught, they would be scourged and burnt through the ear. If they were found begging again within 60 days they would be hanged.

EVIL DOARIS

In the years after Flodden there was much anarchy in the streets of Edinburgh. In order to restore order to the capital we are told that in 1515 . . .

'Evil doaris were punnesit, among the qukilkis ane Peter Moffat, ane greit rever and theif was heit and for exampill of utheris his head wes put on the West Port of Edinburgh.'

LADY LOTHIAN'S MOVABLE CANCER

Lady Lothian's son-in-law Sir Alexander Hamilton was lying in Prestongrange pertaining to the Abbey of Newbattle when he was dragged out of bed by a group of witches and 'sore beaten'. He complained of his injury to Lady Lothian. He told her he intended to complain to the council. However, she promptly pacified him with a purse of gold.

Shortly after, Lady Lothian developed a cancer in her breast. She sought the assistance of a notable warlock named Playfair. He agreed to rid her of her cancer but only on the condition that 'the sore should fall on them that she loved best'.

She recovered but her husband, the earl, developed a boil

in his throat of which he died shortly thereafter. Playfair was then arrested and imprisoned. He confessed all to the Revd Archibald Simson. Robert, Earl of Lothian, heard of the confession and had the means to get some men admitted to 'speak' with Playfair during the night.

Next morning, Playfair was found strangled by his own trousers. No investigation was made as to who might have been responsible for the murder.

THE BURNING OF LADY GLAMMIS

In 1539, Jane Douglas, sister of the Earl of Angus and widow of John Lyon Lord Glammis, her son Gillespie Campbell, her second husband, Lord Lyon (a relation of her first husband), and an old priest were accused of attempting to poison King

Edinburgh Castle, as it was before the siege in 1573

James V. Such an accusation upon this family was strange since they lived constantly in the country far away from court. Their relatives and servants were thoroughly questioned but, even when tortured, nothing to the detriment of the family could be extorted. Nevertheless they were condemned and confined in Edinburgh Castle.

On the appointed day the beautiful and unfortunate Lady Glammis was led from the castle gates and chained to a stake. Barrels tarred and faggots oiled were piled around her, and she was burned to ashes within view of her son and husband, who beheld the terrible scene from the tower that overlooked it.

Lady Glammis was burnt alive on the Castle Hill, greatly pitied by the spectators. Her rank, her blooming youth and uncommon beauty affected the mob so deeply that they all burst into tears and uttered 'loud lamentations' for her untimely end.

The next day, her husband in endeavouring to escape from the castle, fell violently to his death, the rope by which he was descending being too short. His body was dashed to pieces among the rocks.

Only at this point did the accuser, William Lyon, another relation of the family, confess to treachery. Realising the horrific effects of his falsehoods, he repented to the king and confessed to his offence. The king was furious. He would neither alter the punishments nor restore any of the confiscated estates.

The son of Lord Glammis, being too young to be involved, was confined in the castle till the king's death in 1542, when he was finally liberated and allowed to take possession of his ancient hereditary estates.

KEPT APART

A feud existed between the Earl of Rothes and Lord Lindsay. Their animosity had been building up for some time until one day in 1520 they accidentally met in the High Street. Both men were accompanied by their followers. They attacked each other and could not be separated until they were both arrested. To prevent a further repetition one of the protagonists was locked up in Dunbar Castle, the other in Dumbarton Castle.

THE MASTER OF FORBES

For the reign of James V the Master of Forbes was confined as a prisoner in Edinburgh Castle. He had been branded a traitor by George, Earl of Huntly, for plotting to murder the king by shooting him with a pistol in Aberdeen. Forbes was also accused by the Earl of Huntly of being the leader of a mutiny of Scottish troops at Jedburgh when the Scottish army was marching on England.

The Master of Forbes protested his innocence and offered to do single combat with the earl. On 31 July 1537 the earl put up a bond of 30,000 merks to show commitment to his accusations.

The combat did not take place but Forbes was brought to trial on 11 July 1538, before Argyle, the Lord Justice General. On the weakest of evidence and the poorest of witnesses the Master of Forbes was sentenced by the Commissioners of Justiciary and fifteen other men of noble rank to be hanged, drawn, beheaded and dismembered on the Castle Hill. As was the custom for traitors his quarters were displayed above the city gates as a warning to all.

FIGHTING THE FRENCH

Any reader of Scottish history is doubtless acquainted with countless stories of friction between Scots and Englishmen. Less common are street battles between the subjects of the Auld

Mary of Guise

Alliance. While collectively we always preferred Frenchmen to Englishmen, there have been individual cases when even those from across the North Sea have had to be put in their place.

During the minority of Mary Queen of Scots, when the young queen was being raised in France and her mother, Mary of Guise, was in charge in Scotland, all was not well in Edinburgh.

Ten thousand Scottish troops were mustered on the Boroughmuir; the English had been starved out of the country, 'For the pest and hunger was rycht evill amongis tham, quha mycht remayne na langer thairin.' So with no enemy to deal with, the Scottish troops and their allies began to quarrel with one another.

It appears that there was a little contretemps between some Scotsmen and a few Frenchmen in the centre of town. Apparently a French soldier fell into a fight with a native in the High Street. The two men came to blows and a number of citizens decided to join in. The aim of these new belligerents was to transport the Frenchman to prison. However, a group of French soldiers who appeared on the scene did not wish this to happen.

At this point James Hamilton, Lord of Stenhouse, Captain of the Castle and Provost of the town, arrived at the fracas with a company of troops. The French soldiers became so angry that they shot their harquebusses quite indiscriminately. A number of people — men, women, and children — were slain outright, including Provost Hamilton and Master William Stewart, 'a gentleman of good reputation'.

The result was that the entire population of Edinburgh conceived a great grudge and hatred against all the Frenchmen who were in the city at the time. Many revenge killings took place during the following weeks.

On one occasion a large group of Frenchmen were driven by the citizens from the Mercat Cross to the head of Niddry's Wynd. There the Frenchmen rallied and were joined by a number of their fellow soldiers. They were again forced to retreat until they reached the Netherbow where they were met by the new Provost and a band of citizens. Yet again, the Provost, his son and various other citizens, women as well as men were slain. The French troops kept possession of the town from five till seven o'clock at night when they returned to the Canongate.

To finally bring peace to the city, the Frenchman who began the trouble in the first place was hanged at the Mercat Cross so that the quarrel between the nations ended where it had begun.

ROBIN HOOD

Around the time of the Reformation in 1560 the frequently re-enacted play *Robin Hood* was sharply called into question. This was a popular game played in honour of pagan gods and heroes of great antiquity. The origin of the game is obscure but in Edinburgh it had been played for many centuries. During the Middle Ages, Robin Hood, a more modern hero, became the principal character.

On 21 June 1561 a number of craftsmen and apprentices met to revive the play. The magistrates were not consulted — an unforgivable oversight as the play had for a number of years been condemned by law. Magistrates removed some weapons and flags but returned them after the mob became threatening. The magistrates then seized James Gillon, a shoemaker as one of the ringleaders. He was accused and tried on the charge of stealing 10 shillings and was condemned to be hanged.

The deacon of crafts used all his influence to persuade the magistrates not to hang Gillon. John Knox's help was even sought but he refused to be involved. The gallows were erected near the Cross; preparations were made for the execution. However, the mob decided to intervene. Rioters assembled in their hundreds, weapons were gathered and passed around, the gallows were broken down and the magistrates were put to flight and pursued vigorously by the mob. Speedily they took refuge in a writer's booth but were virtually besieged by the mob. The Tolbooth was then attacked. The door was broken down with sledge hammers and Gillon was set at liberty. The mob dispersed, another just

John Knox

cause having been successfully fought for and the magistrates now moved to the Tolbooth for greater safety.

The deacons of trades were summoned to rescue the Provost and baillies 'but they had past to their four hours penny' or afternoon pint; replying to the summons 'that since they will be magistrates alone, let them rule alone'. In other words the magistrates had got themselves into this mess so they could get themselves out of it. The Provost then sought help from the Governor of the Castle.

At this point it should be noted that the City Fathers on many occasions resented the presence of the military in their city. The soldiers of the monarch were tolerated as long as they did not at any time attempt to pull rank or act contrary to the wishes of the Council. Consequently the Governor of the Castle was reluctant to get involved in any domestic dispute between the Edinburgh people and their civil rulers. Therefore no great onslaught was made on the mob by the military.

Meanwhile the rioters did not fully disperse and in the evening reassembled to gloat at their captives in the Tolbooth and to prevent any escape which might be attempted. The Council was finally allowed its freedom when a proclamation was issued saying that no one would be prosecuted for the violence of that day.

THE DISPERSAL OF JAMES HAMILTON

In 1541 James Hamilton, the bastard son of the Earl of Arran, was accused of breaking into the king's chamber, with the intention of murdering him. He was doubly accused of carrying on a secret correspondence with the Douglases who as a family were pretty much public enemy number one at the time.

Hamilton was condemned to death, beheaded and quartered at the Mercat Cross. As was customary the different parts of his body were affixed to the most public places of the city for all to see.

TWA ENGLISHCES

Equally tragic as the demolition of the Tolbooth in 1817 was the removal of the Mercat Cross by the magistrates of Edinburgh in 1756. Although rebuilt with great accuracy at the behest of William Gladstone, the Prime Minister in 1885, no reconstruction can hold the history of the original.

From its top, around its shaft, royal proclamations, solemn denunciations of excommunication and outlawry involving ruin and death were announced year upon year. It was a location of the strange and the terrible, the brutal and the bizarre.

To get a true flavour of one of its principal functions the following extract is quoted from Nicolls diary:

'Last September, 1652. Twa Englisches, for drinking the King's health, were takin and bund at Edinburgh croce, quhait wither of thame resauit thirty-nine quhipes on thut naked bakes and shoulderis; thairafter their lugs were naillit to the gallows. The one had his lug cuttit from the ruitt with a razor, the other being also naillit to the gibbet and his mouth skobit, and his tong being drawn out the full length, was bound together betwirxt two sticks, hard togedder, with a skainzio-thrid, for the space of half one hour thereby.'

A PILLORIED PRIEST

Sir James Cravet, a Roman Catholic priest, was arrested for reading mass in 1564. The citizens of Edinburgh arrayed him in his sacerdotal robes. Fixing a chalice in his hand, they mounted him upon and tied him to the Mercat Cross. They left him there for an hour during which time he was pelted by the mob with rotten eggs and any other similar (or not so similar) materials. On the next day he was exposed in the same place for four hours. With the hangman in attendance Sir James was even more severely treated than on the previous day.

Queen Mary, imagining this to have been done in contempt of her and their religion, wrote to her friends in the country, to march with their respective forces to Edinburgh with the utmost speed and destroy the city. This may seem to the reader a rather drastic action to save a pilloried priest but Mary took religion very seriously.

The magistrates, being informed that their enemies at court were endeavouring to persuade the queen that many of the principal citizens had been concerned in throwing missiles at Cravet, sent a deputation to Mary at Stirling. They attempted to 'undeceive' her and to give her a full and faithful account of how Cravet had been convicted, as well as of their own behaviour. They must have convinced her for, while the priest was still on the pillory, the queen countermanded the march of the troops to the city.

The priest and the city were both saved.

The Mercat Cross

AN EXPENSIVE BUSINESS

It is often the case in history that when great issues are at stake, those in authority preoccupy themselves with trivia. Thus it was in 1567. That year witnessed the capture and incarceration of Mary Queen of Scots in Loch Leven Castle, her subsequent and enforced abdication, the miscarriage of twins by her majesty and the proclamation of Prince James as King James VI at the age of 13 months and 10 days.

To Edinburgh Town Council these matters were of little consequence when compared with 'Fornication'. It appears that in the eyes of the baillies and magistrates there was altogether too much of it going on in the capital. New punishments for offenders were introduced, for example, being ducked in filthy and stagnant pools, being confined in the most dark, dank and dismal cells of the dungeon and being placed on a diet of bread and water.

It also appears that many of their sanctions received royal assent and became legislation. There is one that the king felt gracious enough to pass at the tender age of a year and a half.

It is statute and ordained be oure Soveraine Lord, with advice and consent of his dearest Regent and the three Estaites of this present parliament, that gif ony person, or personis within his realme, to burgh or to land, sall commit the filthie vice of fornication, and beis convict thereof, that the committeris thereof, sall be punished in maner following.

That is to say, for the first fault, alsweill the man as the woman, sall pay the summe of fourtie pundes: or then baith he and she, sall be imprisoned for the space of aucht dayes, their fude to be breade and small drinke, and thereafter presented to the mercat place of the toune or parochin bairheaded, and there stand fastened, that they may not remove, for the space of twa houres; as fra ten houres to twelve houres at noone.

For the second fault being convict, they sall pay the summe of ane hundred markes, or then the foirnamed dayis of their imprisonment sall be doubled, their fude to be bread and water allanerlie. And in the end, to be presented to the said mercat place, and baith the headis of the man and the woman to be schaven.

And for the third fault, being convict thereof, sall pay ane hindreth pundis, or else their above imprisonment to be triples, their fude to be breade and water allanerlies. And in the end, to be tane to the deipest and foullest pule, or water of the toune, or parochin, there to be thrise dowked, and theirafter banished the said toune or parochin for ever. And fra thence furth how oft that every they be convict, of the foresaid vice of fornication that sa oft the said third penaltie be execute upon them.

THE MURDER OF BAILLIE MACMORRAN

Halfway up the Lawnmarket in the inner part of Riddell's Close stands the house of Baillie John Macmorran whose tragic death in 1595 caused a great stir at the time, threw the city into painful excitement and almost ruined the reputation of the famous old High School. The behaviour of the scholars there had been bad and turbulent for some years, but it reached a climax on 15 September 1595.

The boys of the High School were permitted only five school holidays a year, all of which fell in May. It was the periodic custom for the boys to band together and make protestations to their masters for an extra week's holiday. It was equally the custom for the request to be refused.

Such was the case in September 1595. On the week's holiday being refused the boys became so exasperated, being chiefly 'gentilmane's bairns' that they formed a compact for vengeance in the true spirit of the age. Armed to the teeth with swords and pistols, they took possession of the school which was at that time in Blackfriars Gardens, refusing entrance to the masters or anyone else. They prepared for a siege.

Baillie Macmorran's House

The doors were barricaded and strongly guarded by some of the boys. All efforts to storm the citadel failed. All attempts at reconciliation floundered. The Town Council lost patience and sent Baillie John Macmorran, one of the wealthiest merchants in the city, to deal with the matter. The boys became outrageous, shouted abuse at the officials, daring them to approach at their peril.

William Sinclair, the son of the chancellor of Caithness appeared as the self-styled leader of this band of desperados. Standing at the window of one of the entrances, which the baillie had ordered his officers to force using a long beam as a battering ram, he proclaimed a final warning to the baillie.

As with the previous ones, this warning went unheeded. Sinclair fired his pistol and slew the baillie on the spot, the ball striking him right in the centre of his forehead. Panic-stricken the boys surrendered. Some immediately ran from the scene of the murder. Others were thrown in jail.

Macmorran's family were too rich to be bribed. They demanded revenge. They demanded blood. But, 'friends threatened death to all the people of Edinburgh if they did the child any harm, saying they were not wise who meddled with scholars, especially gentlemen's sons.' Lord Sinclair, William's uncle and head of the family, procured the intercession of King James VI with the magistrates of Edinburgh.

In the end all the accused were set free including young Sinclair the murderer, after it was made clear that the nobility would transfer their children to another school. Someone had to be punished however for bringing the school into disrepute. Of course it was the teachers' fault. The headmaster, Hercules Rollocks, was dismissed and the masters received an instant reduction in salary.

THE REVENGE OF A GENTLEMAN

On Sunday 2 April 1600, Robert Auchmutie, barber, slew James Wauchope in a duel in St Leonards Hill. On 3 April

Robert was locked up in Tolbooth Jail. While he was incarcerated he hung a cloak outside the windows of the iron house and used another to cover the windows from the inside saying that as he was ill he didn't want any bright light in the room. While the windows were thus covered from view, we are told 'he had aquafortis continually seething at the iron windows'. Eventually the iron bars were eaten through. In the morning he summoned the apprentice boy who came and waited. By a waving of his hand the boy gave his master the signal that the guard had disappeared.

Robert then dropped out a tow rope on which he planned to descend. However, the guard saw the young boy wave his hand and so Robert's plan failed.

On 10 April 1600, Robert Auchmutie was beheaded at the Cross upon the scaffold especially on the orders of the king for having presumed to take the revenge of a gentleman.

The Tolbooth

PRESENTED AT THE BAR

In the year of the Union of the Crowns, 1603, Francis Maubray was charged with the most high, horrible and detestable points of treason. Prior to his trial he was incarcerated in Edinburgh Castle. However, during his time behind bars he attempted to escape. The attempt was unsuccessful for Maubray was killed. It might be imagined that that would have been the end of the story. But on this occasion a royal warrant was directed to the court of justiciary setting forth the deceased's crimes.

Although Maubray had obstinately and persistently denied the charge there were apparently two or three witnesses who verified it. The fact that he had tried to escape only confirmed his supposed guilt.

The warrant required the court to pronounce a sentence on the deceased. Thus Francis Maubray was presented at the bar — his dead body was literally brought into the court. The trial took place. Maubray was found guilty and the sentence pronounced. He was to be dismembered as a traitor, his body to be hung on a gibbet and thereafter quartered. His head and limbs were to be stuck on conspicuous places in the city of Edinburgh and his whole estate forfeited.

Doom was pronounced accordingly and the sentence put into execution.

ADULTERY

Adultery first became a capital offence in the reign of Mary Queen of Scots although its introduction was more to do with her High Kirk Minister, John Knox, than herself. For this was the time of the Protestant Reformation. The laws against adulterers were extended by her son, James VI.

Thus in 1617 John, Laird of Guthrie, was prosecuted for adultery. He was accused of having married in Forfarshire and deserted his wife, moving to Leith and changing his name to Guthrie. He then married again, living with his second wife for several years. 'These facts', we are told, 'he acknowledged before the Kirk Session and did penance in sackcloth for his impurities.'

A warrant under the royal signature was dated at Whitehall, 26 January 1617, and directed to the Lord Justice General. Guthrie was taken to the Mercat Cross and hanged on a gibbet until he was dead.

On the same day Alexander Thomson and Janet Cuthbert were, by virtue of a royal warrant, tried, convicted and condemned to be hanged for the same crime.

However, the king out of 'princely clemency' commuted their punishment to banishment for life.

MONTROSE AND ARGYLL

It is one of the great truisms of history that justice has little to do with right or wrong but on which side a victim happens to be at the time. In the turbulent history of seventeenth century Scotland what was the 'right' side in one decade could be the 'wrong' in the next.

So it was in the cases of two of our most noble lords, the Marquis of Montrose and the Earl of Argyll, both of whom met their fate in Edinburgh.

In 1650 the Marquis of Montrose returned to Scotland at the head of a small Royalist army. By this time Oliver Cromwell (who may be regarded as a hero south of the border but is definitely a villain in Scotland) was firmly established as Lord Protector. Any attempt to restore Charles II was therefore treason and would be dealt with accordingly. Montrose was already a condemned man, the death sentence having been passed on him six years earlier for his support of Charles I.

Montrose and his army met government forces at the Battle of Carbisdale and had the great misfortune to lose. Thus, this prized prisoner was carried off to Edinburgh to receive the punishment he had long evaded.

He was 'to be carried to Edinburgh Cross, and hanged up,

on a Gallows Thirty Feet high for the space of three hours, and then to be taken down, and his head to be cut off upon a scaffold and hanged on Edinburgh Tolbooth, his legs and arms to be hanged up in other Towns of the Kingdom.'

Prior to this dramatic conclusion to his life the prisoner, Montrose, was taken in procession through the town to be ridiculed and taunted by the citizens of Edinburgh who can always be trusted to put on a good show on such occasions. We are told that it was with great dignity that he received the jeers and abuse from his old enemy, the Earl of Argyll, as the procession passed by his residence of Moray House. The ever charming Countess of Argyll is reported to have spat in Montrose's face as the cart stopped directly outside her window.

However, almost eleven years to the day, the spirit of Montrose got its revenge. In 1660 the monarchy was restored and Charles II became king. Among the old scores which had to be settled was the fate of none other than the Earl of Argyll, whose support of Cromwell's Commonwealth cost him his life. He was tried in the city, condemned to death and sent to the castle prison to await execution where he had much time to think up his last words to the world before hastily departing. 'I could die as a Roman but choose rather to die as a Christian,' Argyll said to the assembled crowd. After his death his head was fixed on a pole above the Tolbooth where it was left to rot.

THE MOORISH PIRATE

There is an ancient tenement in the Canongate adorned by a curious turbaned moor occupying a pulpit. Various romantic stories are told of the character after whom the area was named Morocco Land. This tale takes us back to the time of the grandson of Mary Queen of Scots.

Soon after the accession of Charles I, a number of tumultuous outbreaks took place on the streets of Edinburgh. On one occasion the provost was assaulted by the mob, his house was broken into and fired and mob rule was soon completely established in the town. When order was finally restored several of the ringleaders were arrested — one of whom was Andrew Gray, younger son of the Master of Gray.

Notwithstanding the exertions of powerful friends, such was the influence of the provost that young Gray was condemned to be executed. But that very night he escaped by means of a rope and a file conveyed to him by a faithful vassal, who had previously drugged a posset for the sentinel. A boat lay at the foot of one of the neighbouring closes. He was ferried over the Nor Loch long before the town gates were opened the following morning. A lessening sail near the mouth of the Firth told the watchful eye of his vassal that Andrew Gray was safe.

Effigy of the Moor, Morocco Land

Years passed and by 1645 Edinburgh had become preoccupied by the plague. Grass grew around the Mercat Cross. The High Street was no longer a busy thoroughfare. Even debtors incarcerated in the Tolbooth were set free. It was said that of the Edinburgh citizens 'scarcely 60 men were left capable of defending the town against attack.'

In the midst of this a large armed vessel of curious form was seen sailing up the Firth, anchoring at Leith. Experienced seamen said that it was an Algerian rover. A detachment of crew landed, made their way to the capital and entered the Canongate. They demanded admission to the city at the Netherbow Port. The magistrates parlied with the leader and offered to ransom the city, warning them of the scourge which presently was ravaging the inhabitants. All, however, was in vain.

The provost, Sir John Smith, withdrew to discuss the matter with citizens of influence. They volunteered large contributions which when amassed should have proved tempting to the pirate king. The provost returned to the Netherbow Port to resume negotiations. The large sum was accepted but only on condition that the son of the provost should be handed over to the corsairs. An impossible request. Why? Because the provost only had a daughter and she was dying of the plague. There was immediately a change in attitude by the Moorish leader. He went off to confer with his men. Their assembly was brief. On his return the pirate announced that he possessed an elixir of wondrous potency and demanded that the provost's daughter be entrusted to his skill. If he did not cure her, he would embark immediately with his men and free the city without ransom.

After further considerable parley, the provost proposed that the leader should enter the city and stay at his own house. The pirate leader refused and rejected all offers of high ransom. Sir John Smith, urged by friends, agreed to the moor's offer. The fair invalid was borne on a litter to the house at the head of the Canongate where the moor had taken up residence. Within a few days the young girl was returned to full health.

There is a rather intriguing denouement to this story. The

Moorish leader and physician was in fact Andrew Gray. It appears that after he escaped from the Tolbooth he was captured by pirates and sold as a slave. He won favour with the Emperor of Morocco and rose in rank and wealth. He then returned to Scotland bent on revenge when to his surprise he found in the object of his vengeance a relative of his own — for Sir John Smith's brother-in-law was Sir William Gray, a kinsman of the Moorish pirate.

The rest of the story can be told briefly. Gray married the provost's daughter and settled down a wealthy citizen in the burgh of the Canongate. The house where he cured the fair patient remained his own and is still adorned with an effigy of his royal patron, the Emperor of Morocco.

IN THE WRONG JOB

Hangman's Craig in the Queen's Park near Samson's Ribs is so called because it was the scene of the suicide of Edinburgh's Common Hangman during the reign of Charles II.

The hangman had not been bred to the job. He was the son of a respectable family with estates in Melrose, but like so many of the well-to-do young men he had led a profligate youth squandering all his patrimony. By the time he reached adulthood he was greatly reduced in circumstances. These dire straits forced him to accept the post of Common Hangman of Edinburgh. This was a particularly obnoxious job because of the number of innocent and religious men who were hanged at this time of ecclesiastical strife.

Constantly trying to conceal his identity and unable to give up many of his old ways and haunts to suit his new social status, he would frequently adorn the garb of a gentleman. One day while mingling with the citizens who played golf at Bruntsfield Links he was recognised. At this he was driven away with shouts of execration and loathing. In despair he threw himself from the crag near Samson's Ribs and perished.

ONLY A BISHOP

Two great ecclesiastical friends in the middle of the seventeenth century were Archbishop Sharp of St Andrews and Bishop Honyman of Orkney.

On 11 July 1668 the two bishops met at the lodgings of the Primate's brother-in-law in the High Street. The coach of the archbishop waited at the door. But by that door stood also 'a lean, hollow-cheeked man, of a truculent countenance'. The man was James Mitchell, a most desperate villain, who, having shaken off all fear of God and respect to man, had plans to murder.

The two clerics prepared to enter the coach. Archbishop Sharp entered first and began to distribute some money to the poor folk in the street. Bishop Honyman placed his hand on the door of the coach to assist his entry. From behind the coach stepped the wicked Mitchell; he shot the Bishop of Orkney beneath his right hand and broke his left arm a little above the wrist with five bullets from his pistol.

Immediately the culprit ran from the top of Blackfriars Wynd, crossed the road and disappeared into the buildings opposite — but not before Archbishop Sharp had caught sight of the man's face.

The mob, ever present on such occasions, registered their great disappointment at this attempted assassination when they discovered that they had been cheated out of witnessing the murder of an archbishop and so they dispersed making no attempt to locate the would-be assassin.

Great indignation was aroused amongst the governing and religious circles throughout Scotland. Indeed a thousand merks were offered for the capture of the villain. This sizeable reward was as much caused by the attempted assassination on Archbishop Sharp — who was the object of the murder — as by the eventual death of Bishop Andrew Honyman. As the bullets resulted in inflicting blood-poisoning the wound never healed and so became fatal.

But what of Mitchell? After the shot was fired he walked rapidly away and escaped into the house of a Presbyterian minister who was out of favour with the church. Later he joined a party of anti-government troops who were subsequently defeated in the Pentland Hills, to the south of the capital. He then escaped to Holland, remained there for five years, returned to Edinburgh and rented a shop within a few doors of Archbishop Sharp's lodgings, where he sold tobacco and groceries.

For a time all was well. But one day it happened that the archbishop saw him. Of course an arrest followed, and on his person were found two loaded pistols. He was tried before the Privy Council, but the evidence was not clear that he was the man. However, upon a promise of anonymity he confessed to the crime.

Some time later, the archbishop had the Privy Council reconvene. Mitchell was put on trial and this time, owing to his confession, he was condemned to death.

On 18 January 1678 James Mitchell was executed in the Grassmarket. In his last speech on the scaffold he said: 'I acknowledge my particular and private sins have been such as merited a worse death than this.' As a matter of fact his private sins were bad. Nevertheless, the manner of his conviction proved a stain upon Archbishop Sharp.

However, this stain did not remain upon his person and character for long. A year after the execution of Mitchell, Archbishop Sharp was finally assassinated. While riding in his coach with his daughter near St Andrews, he was slain by nine Covenanters. After shots had been fired which wounded him, he fell out of the coach. Upon bended knee, praying for his life, he was ruthlessly struck to the ground, beaten to death and a sword thrust through his body.

PUNISHMENT FOR BANKRUPTCY

'Order for the wearing of apparel of a Bankrupt.

Debtors to sit on a pillary of hewn stone, near the Mercat Cross on a Market day, from 10 am till one after dinner. Before coming out of Tolbooth [bankrupt] must provide at own cost, flat cap of yellow colour to be worn while sitting on pillary.

Liable to three months imprisonment if found wanting said bonnet or cap.

If bankrupt does not stay at stone he is liable to be arrested by creditors.'

ALL IN WHITE

On the first of December 1680 James Skeen, Archibald Stuart and John Potter were tried and convicted of treason against the king. They were condemned to be hanged at the Mercat Cross. On the day of the execution Skeen appeared completely clothed from head to toe in white linen right down 'to his very shoes and stockings, in affectation of purity and innocence' to prepare himself for the white robe he would receive in Heaven.

As was the custom the heads were stuck on the West Port gate. Inexplicably the heads were stolen three months later.

BURNING THE POPE

Christmas Day in 1680 was 26 December, not the 25th. On that day scholars of the College of Edinburgh decided to band together to make an effigy of the Pope. They made a pact to hold a solemn procession. The band was secured by a jointly taken oath of secrecy and the climax was to be the public burning of the effigy.

News of this reached the town council. Orders were given to bring the king's forces into the city. They were to seize some of the English boys (considered to be the ringleaders) and to imprison them in the Tolbooth. All of this was achieved but the procession continued. They marched up to the Castle Hill carrying a portrait of the Pope. The king's forces were ready for them. They drew up at the West Bow and in the Grassmarket to prevent their escape, but the boys raced off down through the closes on the north side leading to the Nor Loch.

Were the boys defeated in their pact? Not at all. The real

Blackfriars Wynd

procession with the true effigy was at the same time being carried from the High School Yards to the head of Blackfriars Wynd and out on to the High Street. They bombarded the effigy with dirt, set fire to the powder within the trunk of the body and left, jubilant at outwitting the town council and royal troops.

An interesting postscript to this story exists. A fortnight later the home of Provost Sir James Dick burned down. Although he had frequently talked of demolishing Mansion House in Priestfield and rebuilding it, Sir James firmly blamed the college boys for this act of arson. It was as provost that Sir James had imprisoned many of them for burning the effigy of the Pope.

Many of his fellow councillors believed such an idea was nonsense because these boys were not fire-raisers. Burning an effigy and burning a house were not the same thing at all. However the Privy Council thought fit by proclamation to shut up the College of Edinburgh and banish the boys to 15 miles outside the city unless their parents sent a letter assuring their future good behaviour.

In defence of the boys, some cried out 'Shall the succeeding generation be starved of good education because in a Protestant country the children in mockery burnt the Pope?'

When the Privy Council thought more deeply about the matter the College was reopened and the boys came back to school.

PRESS-GANGED

In May 1682 a riot ensued in Edinburgh lasting two days. Johnston, son of the Town Major of Edinburgh was a lieutenant in the Dutch service. He and some officers seized a group of trades apprentices and persuaded them to be soldiers in the service of the Prince of Orange. The soldiers were chiefly after those who had committed a civil disturbance in the recent past and had been imprisoned by Major Johnston. The apprentice friends of those imprisoned fell on Major Johnston, beat him

The Netherbow Port from the High Street

severely and made him promise that he should set free their incarcerated colleagues.

However, Major Johnston got some of the king's forces to take the prisoners to Leith to transport them.

On their way to Leith some women and tradesmen cried to the young men: 'Pressed or not pressed?' When they answered that they were being press-ganged the crowd began to throw stones and any other available missiles at the military. As they approached the Netherbow Port the rabble attacked them from the streets, the windows and the houses which were being built at the time. 'The king's forces were exceedingly assaulted and abused.'

Major Keith ordered his troops to fire. Between ten and twelve innocent bystanders were shot. The crowd now heard that the Privy Council was meeting in Sir George Kinnaird's rooms. They went and threw stones at the glass windows. Three were arrested. His Majesty's Advocate decided to hang them as an example to the ringleaders. But on 6 May the jury refused to find them guilty.

The magistrates were blamed for not dealing with the trouble and for allowing the king's forces to enter the town thus allowing more blood to be shed than at any time during the previous 60 years.

Finally, the Provost and the Dean of the Guild (as head of the merchants and the apprentices) were bound over to help keep the peace under the penalty of 50,000 merks.

ORDEAL BY TOUCH

The Murder of Sir James Stanfield

One of the most popular pubs in the Old Town of Edinburgh is The World's End, opposite the Netherbow. Why it was called 'The World's End' is simply because that's where it was. The Netherbow Gate, a port in that part of the city wall, separated the distinct and different town of the Canongate from the capital. The termination of Edinburgh was to all intents and purposes the end of the world.

To aquaint ourselves fully with the murder of Sir James Stanfield, we must return to a time of blood and superstition, witchcraft and murder, guilt and fear, with of course the finger of God pointing the final way.

Sir James Stanfield was a Yorkshireman by birth. The owner of a substantial property where, and above which, the pub now stands, his main domicile was in New Mills in East Lothian. He settled in Scotland after the victory of Oliver Cromwell at Dunbar, in whose army he had held the rank of Colonel. There at New Mills, a mile east of Haddington, he established a cloth manufactory which prospered greatly under both Cromwell and Charles II.

While Sir James was fortunate and prosperous in business, he was not so in his domestic life. His wife was no help to him. His eldest son, Philip, developed from being a recalcitrant child into a brutish and violent young man. Philip, as a student at the ancient University of St Andrews, earned for himself a degree of notoriety for throwing a substantial object at a minister of the church during a service. (The minister who was the object of this missile was Revd John Welsh, the great-grandson of John Knox.) The minister, obviously a soundly intelligent and quick-witted man, immediately prophesied in front of the assembled congregation that 'there would be more present at [Philip's] death than were hearing him preach that day.'

Accepting all the advantages of an excellent education, Philip became 'a profligate and debauched person [and] did commit and was accessory to several notorious villanies both at home and abroad.' Always he was saved from prisons and severe punishments by his father who received no thanks or thoughts of appreciation. Apparently it was the son's habit 'most wickedly and bitterly to rail upon, abuse and curse his natural and kindly parent.'

By 1686 Sir James's family — Lady Stanfield, Philip and John, the second son who was perpetually drunk — became such a financial liability that he was forced to sell 'the houses and lands of Newmills'. In the meantime, Sir James disinherited Philip, the effect of which can be easily imagined.

Crisis point was reached on 27 November 1687. Sir James, having been in Edinburgh on business, returned to New Mills with a friend, the Reverend John Bell. They dined together and at 10 o'clock the minister retired to bed. The next events are described in the minister's own words:

> I declare that having slept but little, I was awakened in fear by a cry (as I supposed), and being awake, I heard for a time a great dinn and confused noise of several voices, and persons sometimes walking, which affrighted me (supposing there to be evil wicked spirits); put me to arise in the night and bolt the chamber-door further, and to recommend my self by prayer, for protection and preservation, to the majestie of God.

The voices continued to be heard. More shouting took place outside the minister's bedroom window which looked out on to the garden and some water beyond. Believing that all had been caused by evil spirits which did not warrant too much investigation, the reverend finally resumed his slumbers.

Next morning Sir James Stanfield was missing. Some way behind the house the River Tyne flowed beneath a steep bank. Early that Sunday morning a stranger called John Topping saw Philip standing at the riverside, his eyes fixed upon the body of a man floating in the river. Topping asked whose body it was but got no reply.

Half-an-hour after day-break Philip went to see the Reverend Bell. He inquired if the minister had seen his father that morning. He had not. Shortly after, Sir James's body was discovered by a member of the household. The Reverend Bell was said to have remarked, 'If the majestie of God did ever permit the Devil and his instruments to do an honest man wrong, then Sir James Stanfield has received wrong this last night, which the Lord will discuss in His good time.'

When the body was carried by his servants to the house, Philip met them at the door and 'aware that the body should not enter there, for he had not died like a man but like a beast', Sir James was placed in an outhouse. The general opinion that suicide was the cause of death was most vigorously prosecuted by Philip and believed by all around. Within an hour of the recovery of the body Philip had ransacked his father's room, removed his valuables and even transferred the silver buckles from his deceased father's shoes to his own.

The Reverend Bell returned to New Mills on the Sunday evening. The following morning he discovered that Philip had buried his father during the night.

Umphray Spurway, the manager of Sir James's mills, did not believe Sir James had taken his own life. He sent his suspicions to the Lord Advocate, who decided that Spurway and a few others should view the body. If there were no problems, the body should be quickly and quietly returned. When the messenger returned he was intercepted by Philip, who suppressed the letter.

At three o'clock on Monday morning Umphray Spurway was awakened. Looking out of his bedroom window towards Sir James's house, he saw people, horses, and 'great lights' moving around. He arose and inquired of Philip what was taking place. Philip replied that 'having received orders from my Lord Advocate', he was taking the body for internment to Morham Churchyard. This was duly done.

On the following night Spurway was again awakened — this time by two surgeons and three other gentlemen who had orders from the Lord Advocate to exhume the body. Spurway and the group journeyed the three miles to the churchyard, where they met Mr Andrew Melvil, minister of the parish, whose services Philip had dispensed with the previous day. The body was carried into the church where the surgeons conducted the examination by torchlight. Philip himself was present, unwillingly and with imaginable feelings.

When the post-mortem was concluded the surgeons requested that the relatives replace the body in the coffin. This was done deliberately in order to subject Philip to ordeal by touch.

In accordance with the Scots custom, Philip took his father's head, but no sooner had he done so than the horrified onlookers 'did see it darting out blood through the linen from the left side of the neck'.

Philip, astounded, let the head fall, staggered back, wiping his bloody hands upon his clothes. He cried out pathetically for God's mercy and then fainted. The onlookers knew that what they had witnessed was 'God's revenge against murder'.

The trial of Philip Stanfield took place in the High Court of Justiciary on 6, 7 and 8 February 1688. The prosecution was led by the Lord Advocate Dalrymple and Sir George Mackenzie, the 'Bloody Mackenzie' of the Presbyterian faith. It was seldom that Sir George did not call upon God as a witness in some part of his prosecution. Never more so was 'the Divine Majesty' apparent than throughout these proceedings.

'God Almighty himself was pleased to bear a share of the testimonies which we produce: that Divine Power which makes the blood circulate during life, has oftimes in all nations opened a passage to it after death upon such occasions.'

With such forces on the side of the crown, no jury would consider the possible innocence of Philip Stanfield for any length of time.

On 8 February, Philip Stanfield was found guilty by a unanimous verdict. Two weeks later, at the Mercat Cross of Edinburgh, he was hanged upon a gibbet. The tongue which had cursed his 'natural and kindly parent' was cut out and burned upon the scaffold. Philip's right hand which had taken his father's life was cut off and fixed to the East Port of Haddington. His dead body was hung in chains at the Gallow Lee and, finally, 'his name, fame, memory and honours were ordained to be extinct.'

Two incidents which took place at this time gave much mileage to the superstitious. During his hanging the knot of the rope slipped 'whereby his feet and knees were on the scaffold.' The Common Hangman of Edinburgh therefore strangled him which, to the assembled crowd, had a just resemblance of the way his father died.

Application was made for the body to be buried. The Lord Chancellor, however, refused and insisted that it be placed among the other malefactors at the Gallow Lee, 'waving with the weather while their neck will hold.' After only a few days' suspension it was secretly taken down and thrown into a neighbouring ditch, 'among some water as his father's corpse was.' Once more, the body was hung up by order of the authorities, but it was again mysteriously removed and never heard of again.

THE GHOST OF JOHNNY ONE-ARM

Strange though it may seem, it is remarkably infrequent that a member of the justiciary becomes the object of murderous revenge at the hands of a former client. The great exception to this is Sir George Lockhart, the Lord President of the Court of Session.

Beginning a legal career in 1656 Sir George proved himself to be a most able barrister and soon became a man of power and influence. It was he who defended James Mitchell, the intended but unsuccessful assassin of Archbishop Sharp of St Andrews.

In 1685 Lockhart became Lord President of the Court of Session and soon afterwards was appointed a privy councillor. It was around this time that Sir George bought a house in Old Bank Close at the bottom of the Lawnmarket where now stand some hideous Lothian Region Council buildings. Thus all was

Sir George Lockhart

53

well with Sir George Lockhart of Carnwath . . . until he met John Chiesly of Dalry.

John Chiesly came from a wealthy family of burgesses who owned land well outside the city wall in the hamlet of Dalry. In 1688 Chiesly wished to be divorced from his wife (though what arrangements were to be made for the eleven children we know not). Much disputation arose between the couple. Both parties agreed to abide by the arbitration of the court.

Sir George Lockhart, who heard the case, pronounced that £93 per annum should be granted to Mrs Chiesly and the children. Chiesly had wished to give them nothing. He was furious. He swore revenge on the Lord President. It appears that he did not keep his thoughts to himself. We know that he informed an advocate, Mr James Stewart, of his intention, six months before the deed was done.

On Easter Sunday, 31 March 1689, Chiesly rose early to clean and load his pistol. He made his way to the Lawnmarket and waited for the Lord President. He knew the Lord President would journey to St Giles for the Easter Service — and he was right. John Chiesly followed the Lord President all the way down to the High Kirk, sat near him in the church, a pistol secreted inside his jacket, and after the service followed him all the way back. Just as the Lord President was about to enter Old Bank Close, John Chiesly took out his pistol and shot the Lord President dead. Sir George staggered and fell to the ground. The ball had gone through his body and out through his right breast.

Chiesly made no attempt to escape. The Edinburgh mob appeared as always. He boasted to all that he was 'not wont to do things by halves' and that he had 'taught the President how to do justice.' As the crime was so serious, parliament ordered that he should be tortured at the Mercat Cross to determine whether he had any accomplices. In great agony he suffered the thumbscrews and the 'booties' but no names were confessed.

Summarily tried before the Provost of Edinburgh, he was sentenced to be hanged at the Gallow Lee. His right hand, used to fire the pistol, was cut off while he was still alive, and stuck on a spike at the West Port. And the pistol itself, the fatal weapon, was hung round his neck. Suspended in chains he was left to rot.

But the story does not end there. A mystery developed as to who removed the body. It had certainly not been Mrs Chiesly. None knew who had done it nor where the body had been buried, but for nearly 300 years a ghost, who rejoiced in the name of Johnny One-Arm haunted the hamlet of Dalry. Laughing, screaming, screeching hysterically, Johnny One-Arm was seen by many generations of Edinburgh citizens. Indeed up until 1965 did Johnny One-Arm put fear and trembling into the hearts of many ordinary folk.

In 1965, in Dalry, workmen were removing the hearthstone of a cottage in Dalry Park. Behind the stone they found the skeleton of a man with badly broken bones — not crumbled through age but broken by physical violence. A skeleton of a man with no right hand and with a pistol hanging round its neck. This was the body of John Chiesly of Dalry, missing for almost 300 years.

From the moment the body was reburied the ghost of Johnny

Dalry Manor House

55

One-Arm has never been seen again. And so we presume that spirit and body, kept apart for so long, are now together in their final resting place.

THE BOOTIES

'Four pieces of narrow boards nailed together of a competent length for the leg . . . which they wedge so tightly on all sides that not being able to bear the pain, they promise confession to be rid of it . . . '

Morer's Short Account of Scotland, 1679

CONFUSION TO ALL PAPISTS

At the time of great religious dispute in the 1680s, when the Protestant cause had the upper hand, the chief officers of state rather foolishly decided to publicly attend a Roman Catholic mass. The Edinburgh mob, ever guardians of current religious etiquette, became so excited against this papish display that they had themselves a tumult. The wife of Scotland's Chancellor and other individuals of distinction were insulted and harried by the populace as they left the chapel.

One of the rioters, a journeyman baker, was arrested. As punishment the Privy Council ordered that he should be whipped through the Canongate. However, while the officers were putting this order into execution, the mob rescued their comrade, beat the hangman and continued to riot during the night.

The king's foot guards and the soldiers in the castle being called out, fired amongst the mob and killed two men and a woman. On the next day, several of the captive rioters were ordered to be whipped but to make sure there was no recurrence of the previous day's events the council arranged to have musqueteers and pikemen on duty.

At the same time an accusation was lodged against a drummer by two papists, for having said that he could find it in his heart to run them through with his sword. During his trial the drummer vigorously protested that he had meant the mob and not the Roman Catholic gentlemen. It appears that this was rejected by the court — he was shot the next day.

The tumult was ended when a fencing master was dealt with at the Mercat Cross merely for having drunk the king's health in public and coupling the toast with an unwise pronouncement, 'confusion to all papists'.

It would appear that the papists were not so confused that they had forgotten how to perform a hanging — for that's what they did the same day.

A VITIATED BOND

In 1700 John Corse, in the course of transacting a business agreement, decided to alter the word 'myself' to 'himself'. One can imagine the implications of such a situation. So it was that Corse was sentenced by the Court of Session to be taken by the Common Hangman to the Tron Kirk before 11 o'clock on 26 July. This journey was not so that he might complete some religious penitence but so that he would be placed at the door and have his ear nailed to it. There he stood so nailed until the clock of the Tron struck mid-day with the words, 'for his knowledge of and using a vitiated bond' fixed to his breast.

CAPTAIN GREEN

A few years before the Treaty of Union in 1707, the Scots were still smarting from the failure of the Darien Scheme. Many people believed that the failure of this Scottish colony was the result of English interference. In March 1705 an unprecedented but not unrelated event took place which served only to inflame national animosity.

A ship belonging to the African Company was seized in the River Thames. The company was given authority from the government to seize, by way of reprisal, a vessel belonging to the English East India Company. This ship, commanded by Captain Green had been driven by stress of weather into the River Forth.

From the unguarded speeches of the crew during some quarrels over a few cups of rum, Captain Green and his men were suspected, accused and after a full and legal trial convicted of piracy. As if that were not enough, Green and his crew were accused of murdering the entire complement of a Scots vessel in the East Indies.

The evidence by which they were convicted seemed to all to be rather slight and intercessions for royal mercy were made on their behalf. The populace of Edinburgh enraged that the blood of a Scotsman should be spilt unrevenged, assembled in great numbers on the day of execution. A vast mob surrounded the prison. The Privy Council and the magistrates sat for some time to deliberate whether the sentence should be put into execution. The magistrates, aware of the furious intentions of the populace, assured them that three of the convicts were ordered for execution.

The Lord Chancellor happened to leave the Privy Council meeting at about the same time. As he drove past the mob in his coach someone called out, 'that the magistrates had but cheated them, and that the criminals were reprieved.' Their fury was instantly kindled into action. The coach was stopped at the Tron Church by the mob who broke the glass of the carriage and dragged the Chancellor out of it. Happily for the Lord Chancellor, some of his Lordship's friends rescued him before any serious damage was done.

It was clear that it was now doubly necessary to appease the multitude by the blood of the criminals. Captain Green and two of his crew were hanged, then everyone went home.

CHILD MURDER

In the first year of the eighteenth century an Edinburgh woman murdered the child of one of her neighbours. During her trial she confessed that she was consumed with hatred, spite and disgust for the child. Continually filled with revengeful thoughts and designs of mischief, the Devil finally appeared to this woman. Over the following days Satan frequently haunted her. He told her that the only way to be at ease and rid herself of her revengeful thoughts was to go and kill the child, which she did. The Devil was right. The woman was put at ease. She was executed the following week.

A MACABRE FEAST

The authors acknowledge the kind permission of the *Scotsman* to reproduce an article from the *Weekly Scotsman*.

Near the foot of the Canongate stands Queensberry House, scene of one of the most horrific events recorded in Edinburgh's chronicles. This tall, gloomy building was troubled from its very foundation in 1680. Charles Maitland of Haltoun, who commissioned the building, chose to employ masons and labourers from the countryside who offered cheaper rates than the craftsmen of the Canongate. Bitterness grew. There were angry exchanges between locals and incomers which culminated in a concerted and violent attack on the intruding countrymen whose tools were carried off by the rioters. Maitland's mansion was eventually completed but only after resort to the law courts.

Maitland's stay in his mansion 'whose very mortar might be said to have been mixed with strife' was a brief one. In 1686 he became the third Earl of Lauderdale and sold 'the great lodging at the foot of the Canongate on the South Side newly built' to William, Lord Drumlanrig, first Duke of Queensberry. Queensberry took possession under duress for he was at that time confined to live within Edinburgh due to his opposition to the pro-Catholic policies of James VII. The Duke supported the revolution against James, and with the accession to the throne of William of Orange, Queensberry joyfully bid farewell to Edinburgh to reside at his country seat at Drumlanrig. He seemed fated to return to the gloom of Queensberry House, however. On the first night at his magnificent country mansion he took violently ill. The following morning, feeling isolated from medical help, he left, never to return, pausing only long enough to curse the house with the phrase, 'The Devil pike out his een that looks herein.'

So began the unhappy association of the Queensberry family with the sombre house which took their name. It was at Queensberry House that the first Duke died in 1695. At the very moment of his death a Scottish seaman in Sicily was startled by a great coach, drawn by six horses hurtling wildly towards the volcanic flames of Mount Etna and heard a Satanic voice bellow, 'Way for the Duke of Drumlanrig.'

The Canongate, Edinburgh, looking west

Flames were to bring tragedy to the Queensberry family on other occasions. Five years after the Duke's death, tragedy struck Queensberry House again. William's daughter, Anne, was alone in her bedroom. Suddenly agonised screams pierced the air. On rushing to her room the servants found Anne in a frenzy, her nightdress ablaze and as she writhed in anguish it was said that, 'Her nose was burnt off and her eyes burnt out. Opening her mouth to call, the flames went in and burnt her tongue and throat.' The rescuers were too late. Her wounds proved fatal.

In 1707, the house was the scene of a macabre feast. There are many versions of the story and here we reproduce an account written early this century in the *Weekly Scotsman*.

James, second Duke of Queensberry, was, like his father, a supporter of William of Orange, who made him a captain in his Dutch Guards and appointed him Lord of the Bedchamber and of the Treasury. He was one of the Commissioners for the drawing up of the Treaty of Union, receiving for his services in this connection the sum of £12,325 along with the additional titles of Duke of Dover, Marquis of Beverley and Baron Ripon. Popular opinion in Edinburgh was, as elsewhere, bitterly opposed to the Union and so strong was the feeling against the Duke of Queensberry that a military guard was necessary for his protection when he emerged from the Parliament House and entered his coach. As he drove down the Canongate to Queensberry House he was pursued by the yells and curses of the angry mob, accompanied by showers of stones and other missiles.

On the day when the Treaty was finally passed all Edinburgh flocked to Parliament Square. Thither too, went the Duke of Queensberry, in all the splendour befitting his high office and attended by his entire household — as much perhaps, for protection as for any other reason.

Down in the deserted Canongate it was very quiet; not a soul walked the cobbled street; not a head was thrust from the high windows. And in the great, stately mansion at the foot of the long brae silence reigned — a most unusual and death-like silence. For the first time since it was built, the huge, rambling house was empty, save for one solitary occupant, the little kitchen boy, who had been left to watch the great roast that spluttered on the spit before the roaring fire, in preparation for the banquet that was to be later in the day.

How the flames crackled as they leaped up the cavernous chimney! When all else was quiet, burning logs seemed to whisper and chuckle, as though they were alive and would fain be companionable.

Suddenly a footstep sounded in the stone-paved corridor; a stealthy, halting footstep, as of one unaccustomed to the place, yet fearful of meeting or being seen by anyone. At the open door of the kitchen the footstep paused for a moment. The boy looked round from his task of turning the spit. There, in the doorway, stood a gigantic figure, with the shape of a man but the attitude of a wild beast; the head was thrust forward and a horrible, leering grin overspread the distorted features, while the murderous alter of a tiger glared from the blood-shot eyes. Two strides and this monster was across the kitchen floor, his claw-like hands had seized the roast and torn it from the spit. Then he flung it down, and turned towards the poor little turnspit who had sprung up in terror from the stool on which he had been sitting, but, paralysed with fright, could move no further. In a moment those long, gaunt arms were holding the boy in a grip of steel. His shrieks were useless, for there was none to hear, and worse than useless was any appeal to the awful creature whose only resemblance to humanity consisted in the shape of his bodily frame.

The jingle of bit and bridle, the tramp of many feet, and the hum of voices — many of them ill-pleased, as the speakers, under their breath, cursed the town rabble that vented its spleen in stone-throwing announced the return of His Grace, the Duke of Queensberry and Dover, Marquis of Beverley and Dumfries, Lord High Commissioner and Lord of the Treasury. Hurriedly the troop of indoor servants resumed their duties, the kitchen staff hastening to complete the culinary preparations of the morning. But the sight that met their eyes was too horrible for description.

In the middle of the kitchen floor lay part of the huge roast which had been left spitted before the fire, though something still smoked on the spit; but the kitchen boy — where was he?

And who or what was this that squatted on the turnspit's stool, devouring, with all the savage gluttony of a beast of prey, a half-roasted piece of . . . Oh! Heaven! could it be —?

The shuddering question was answered by a haggard, terrified manservant, who came running along the passage, wild-eyed and breathless, 'He's gotten oot!'

'Gotten oot?'

'Aye, yon loonie! Oh! Heaven, hae mercy on us!'

His Grace the Duke of Queensberry had title and wealth and power, but of what avail were these when the heir to them all was a rabid, bestial maniac?

For long years the dark secret had been kept, but now it was out. For many years one of the ground-floor rooms of the Queensberry mansion had been the prison-house of a wretched lunatic. In that room, where the windows were half obscured by oaken boards, lest anyone passing by should see what was within, the proud Duke of Queensberry's eldest son had grown from imbecile childhood to the maturity — if such it could be called — of a savage and uncontrollable madman, huge in stature, fierce and gluttonous as a wild animal.

On this particular day the manservant whose sole duty it was to watch over the wretched creature — glad no doubt, to be quit for a brief period of his odious charge — had gone up to Edinburgh with the rest of the household, and in his absence the maniac, breaking the bonds with which he was secured, had somehow managed to open the door of his prison and wander through the empty house. Attracted by the savoury smell of the roast, he had found his way to the kitchen and then ensued the awful tragedy already outlined above.

In 1926 the scene of the tragedy was revealed when the original fireplaces were exposed during restoration work which took place throughout the building.

In 1832 the Queensberry family cut their ties with the house and it became a house of refuge for the destitute. Today it is a hospital but its past is not forgotten. There are those, even today, reluctant to enter the old kitchens after dark, lest they too fall victim to the cannibal of the Canongate.

THE PHANATICK'S GOD

In the summer of 1702 the Town Clerk of Edinburgh was Mr John Spreul. One day his servant had cause to visit the Tolbooth on some court business. While climbing the Tolbooth stair (it being without an iron railing) he was pushed over by the crowd and fell on the causeway below.

Passing by at the time was one, John Walkinshaw.

'Johnny, this is the phanatick's God that has saved you, and keeped your neck from being broke!' he exclaimed.

'Sir, mock not; I was in great danger,' answered the servant.

'Ay,' said Mr Walkinshaw, 'but when you are in the company of phanaticks with their prayers you cannot be hurt.'

The following day, the Sabbath, young Walkinshaw, the eldest son of John, fell down his own stair and smashed his brains out. Clearly the young man had not had a sufficiently phanatickal relationship with God.

EXITS FROM THE TOLBOOTH

The records of the Tolbooth jail make fascinating reading and provide much evidence of those activities considered serious enough to merit a hanging. The seventeenth and eighteenth centuries seem to be the most lively.

1662 June 10 — Robert Binning for falsehood; hanged with the papers around his neck. August 13 — Robert Reid for murder. His head struck from his body at the Mercat Cross. December 4 — James Ridpath, tinker; to be ghupitt (whipped) from Castle-hill to Netherbow, burned on the cheek with the town's common mark, and banished the kingdom, for the crime of double adultery.

1663 March 13 — Alexander Kennedy; hanged for raising false bonds and writs. July 8 — Katherine Reid; hanged for theft. July 8 — Sir Archibald Johnston of Warriston; treason.

Hanged, his head cut off and placed on the Netherbow. July 18 — Bessie Brebner; hanged for murder. October 5 — William Dodds; beheaded for murder.

The rest of the century continues in this vein with relentless monotony.

1728 October 25 — John Gibson; forging. His lug was nailed to the Tron and dismissed. 1756   May 4 — Sir William Dalrymple of Cousland; for shooting at Captain Hen. Dalrymple of Fordell, with a pistol at the Cross of Edinburgh. Liberated on 14 May, on bail for 6000 merks.

1752 January 10 — Norman Ross; hanged and hung in chains between Leith and Edinburgh for assassinating Lady Bailie, sister to Home of Wedderburn.

1757 February 4 — James Rose, Excise officer at Muthill; banished to America for forging receipts for arrears.

It was one of the great peculiarities of the Tolbooth that almost every criminal of rank placed within its walls managed to escape.

Robert, Lord Burleigh, a half insane peer assassinated a schoolmaster who had married a girl to whom the noble lord had paid improper addresses. He was committed to the Tolbooth and sentenced to death. In his first attempt to escape he was packed into a large trunk which was to be transported to Leith on the back of a powerful porter. The trunk was to be delivered to a vessel about to sail for the Continent. Slinging the trunk on his back the head of Lord Burleigh was forced downwards thus having to sustain the weight of his whole body. The position was agonising.

Unconscious of his actual burden, the porter reached the Netherbow Port where he was met by a friend. When asked where he was headed, the porter replied, 'To Leith'. 'Is the work good enough to afford a glass before going farther?' inquired the friend. The porter said it was; and tossed down the trunk with such violence that Lord Burleigh screamed and instantly fainted.

Scared and astounded the porter wrenched open the trunk. The inmate was found cramped, doubled-up and senseless. A crowd gathered, the city Guard appeared and the prisoner was restored to his former quarters.

HALF-HANGIT MAGGIE

In 1723 Margaret Dickson, a fish hawker, was deserted by her husband shortly after the birth of their second son. Utterly distressed she decided to quit Edinburgh for some time and head for Newcastle to stay with some relatives.

She never reached Newcastle. To split her journey she stopped for a night in Kelso and stayed at an inn in the quiet Borders town. She liked the landlady and her family so much that she asked if she could stay for a while and work in return for her board and lodgings. This happiness turned sour. Not only did Margaret form a bond of friendship with Mrs Bell, the landlady, she formed an even stronger one with her son, William. Shortly Margaret found herself in a state of pregnancy.

This was bad news. This was not in her contract of employment. So Margaret hid the fact that she was expecting. Her successful attempts at concealing her condition led to the child being born prematurely. After only a few days the baby died. Margaret determined to throw the baby into the river Tweed which flowed past the hotel. But at the last moment she lost her nerve and instead placed it in some long reeds near the water's edge.

That same day the body was found by a local fisherman who immediately drew his discovery to the attention of the magistrates. Kelso being a small town with everyone knowing everyone else's business, the birth of the child was traced back to Maggie. She was arrested and charged under the 1690 Concealment of Pregnancy Act and returned to Edinburgh for trial. This was a capital offence. Maggie was tried, found guilty and sentenced to death by hanging.

Maggie Dickson had been a popular and well-known figure in Edinburgh's street life. Many thousands turned up for her execution on 2 September 1742. The hanging took place in the Grassmarket. Some friends brought a cart and a coffin to give her a decent burial.

She was hanged. Death was pronounced by the attending doctor and the body was cut down by the hangman. Then all hell let loose! The medical students were out that day and they wanted the body. A great scuffle ensued but the outraged Edinburgh mob gave the students a sound thrashing and secured the body in the coffin.

On the way to Musselburgh where Maggie was to be buried, the funeral party decided to stop off at the Sheep Heid tavern in Duddingston. After an hour or two recounting the virtuous life of the deceased they continued their journey. But just as they turned into the graveyard the funeral party heard muffled moans and groans coming from the coffin.

They opened the lid and found to their astonishment that Maggie was alive! Returned to Edinburgh, Maggie recovered her full health during the following few weeks. But there was a problem. Should she be hanged again? Representatives from the Church, the University and the Town Council debated the issues.

The greatest brains of the day discussed Maggie's future. Lawyers looked for precedents, but in vain. Finally it was decided that as death had been pronounced, any change in those circumstances must be an act of God — and even Edinburgh Town Council dared not challenge the works of the Lord.

Thus Margaret Dickson was set free and lived in Edinburgh for another 40 years — known by all as the celebrated 'Half-Hangit Maggie'.

THE PORTEOUS RIOTS

One day a history of the Edinburgh mob must be written. One of the fiercest in Europe in times past, ever-present to fight for a just cause or to defend their own rights, the populace of the capital must have been a most volatile and fearsome group — not one to be challenged lightly.

Maintaining peace in the city was the responsibility of the City Guard. Old Highlanders, carrying Lochabers, Gaelic speaking, frequently intoxicated, objects of abuse and schoolboy ridicule, they had their headquarters in the middle of the

High Street just west of the Tron Kirk. The poet Fergusson colourfully referred to them as 'that black banditti'.

In 1726 John Porteous was appointed captain of the guard. Porteous was an arrogant and conceited man with a violent temper. He did not suffer fools gladly and would not suffer the Edinburgh mob at all. He boasted of his friendship with Edinburgh's prominent citizens. His appointment was an unfortunate choice.

The animosity between the mob and the City Guard focused on its captain and came to a head in 1736. In March of that year two smugglers, Wilson and Robertson, were sentenced to death for robbing an excise officer in Fife. Smugglers were regarded as popular heroes at this time. Wilson and Robertson were particularly well thought of because of their daring attempts at escape from the Tolbooth.

Three days before their execution the smugglers were taken to the Tolbooth Church, at that time part of St Giles. They went to attend their own funeral service. The church was packed. Just before the service began Robertson suddenly broke loose from his guard. The congregation witnessed the entire event and did everything they could to conceal him in their midst and secure his escape. Wilson also seized hold of the other guards to prevent them pursuing Robertson as he fled through the religious assembly. Wilson was now the man of the hour in the eyes of the mob.

On the day of his execution great preparations were made in the Grassmarket. The authorities feared that the mob would attempt to rescue Wilson. The entire City Guard was on duty. Guns and ammunition had been issued on the orders of the provost. As an extra precaution a detachment of soldiers had been drawn up in the Lawnmarket. This made Porteous furious. It was a gross insult to the City Guard. Porteous took out his anger on Wilson. He was the cause of this effrontery. He would suffer.

When Wilson was removed from the Tolbooth he was manacled for his journey to the scaffold. But the manacles were found to be too small for his wrists. Porteous was told, rushed forward and squeezed them until they shut. He refused to pay the slightest attention to the cries of extreme

The High Kirk of St Giles

pain from the condemned man. News of the torture spread amongst the crowd. A groundswell of hatred spread around the city.

The execution took place at the east end of the Grassmarket. The Guard surrounded the scaffold in case of trouble. But the crowd looked on in silence. Only twenty minutes later, when the hangman began to cut down the body, did the rage of the mob finally come to a head. Stones were hurled at Porteous, who hastily took shelter behind his men.

At that point a relative of Wilson rushed forward to take the body and vainly try to resuscitate it. In order to prevent the Guard interfering in this, the crowd began to stone them, causing a considerable degree of injury.

What followed is shrouded in some confusion and doubt. It is believed that Porteous drew his pistol, fired the first shot and killed a man. The Guard then began to fire into the panic-stricken crowd. Three onlookers were killed outright. Twelve more were wounded — some of whom died later. Some shots which were fired over the heads of the crowd hit spectators in nearby windows. All this happened in only a few moments, at the conclusion of which Porteous and his men marched off.

The mob was now after blood. They followed, shouting angrily and throwing more stones. About halfway up the West Bow the Guard stopped, turned and fired, killing three more and wounding others. Matters had gone too far. The city was outraged. This had not been the action of a man intent on maintaining law and order. This was slaughter. The provost and magistrates had to take action. They did. Captain Porteous and 30 of his men were arrested and he was dismissed from his office. The provost proposed to try Porteous for murder. But it could be said that Porteous was acting upon instructions given to him by the city fathers. And so they were dissuaded by Duncan Forbes, the Lord Advocate, from trying the case on the charge of murder.

On 5 July 1736 the trial of Captain Porteous began at the High Court of Justiciary. Porteous was charged with having ordered his men to fire 'without any just cause or necessary occasion.' The Crown produced 28 witnesses to support their case. Porteous produced 16 to dispute it. By a majority of one Porteous was found guilty. He was sentenced to death.

But Porteous had friends in high places. A large number of his well-connected friends petitioned Queen Caroline for his reprieve. On 2 September a reprieve reached Edinburgh. The people of Edinburgh became indignant. Suspicion existed that London did not wholly disapprove of Porteous's actions.

Reprieve or no reprieve the Edinburgh mob determined to hang him on the previously appointed day, 8 September. The provost hesitated. He believed, or rather hoped, that the mob would only make a commotion outside the Tolbooth and that would be the end of it. Surely the troops in the castle and the Canongate would have been able to deal with any unrest.

Little went according to plan. Outside the West Port a small band of men assembled on 7 September at nine o'clock. They seized the gate and locked it. This was repeated at another gate in the city wall. At a quarter-to-ten the Netherbow Port

The Porteous Riots

was seized and locked. Thus the troops from the Canongate were barred from entering the city.

The door of the Tolbooth jail proved to be more of an obstacle to the capture of Porteous than the mob had bargained for. So they burned it down. Water was at hand to stop the flames from spreading. Every care was taken to do no unnecessary damage to persons or property.

They found Porteous in his cell. Inquiring as to their intentions the mob informed the captain that they were going to carry him to the place where he had shed so much blood and hang him. This they did. By the light of flaming torches they led him up the Lawnmarket, down the West Bow and into the Grassmarket — stopping only once to open up a rope-seller's shop in the West Bow to procure some coils of rope for the deed. Honourable at all times the correct money was left for the owner to find in the morning as payment for the appropriated wares.

A little before midnight Captain Porteous was hanged by the neck until truly dead.

THE CAT NICK CHASM

In 1770 Mungo Campbell committed suicide in the Tolbooth while under sentence of death for the murder by shooting of the Earl of Eglinton. Nevertheless, his body was dragged through the streets by the mob, who threw it from the summit of Salisbury Crags into the chasm known as the Cat Nick.

BOWED JOSEPH

We read much of the Edinburgh mob in the dark annals of the capital's past. Of its leadership we know much less. One exception is during the decade 1770 to 1780. For at that time the undisputed ring leader was Bowed Joseph, an ill-shapen cobbler who was able to rally his troops at the beat of his drum whenever a just cause had to be fought for.

It must be understood by the reader that the mob was not simply a collection of parochial terrorists. Their actions were always based on justice — or at least their interpretation of it — and pervaded by a cynical sense of humour and irony that have always been so much a part of Scottish culture.

Bowed Joseph's muster point was at Old Assembly Close on the site of the old well. This was a convenient location for his frequent assaults on the City Chambers to worry the provost and baillies after their most recent piece of legislation had met with Joseph's disapproval. Mounted on a water stoup, beating his drum to draw his followers, he reigned like a king. A cross between Robert the Bruce and Robin Hood, Joseph's magnetic power placed him at the head of a loyal army which, had the Young Pretender been able to call on their services, the course of British history might have been quite different.

So great was his authority he could collect or disperse 10,000 people in an hour. Always on the rampage against foul play he thought nothing of besieging the town council in their chambers.

If a High Street landlord thought to charge an unfair rent, Joseph and the mob would ransack the property, pile the furniture in the middle of the street and set fire to the lot. In times of social and economic hardship he would compel all Grassmarket meat dealers to sell their meat at reasonable prices to the poor. Joseph, of course, would determine what was a reasonable price.

On a number of occasions, the town council, believing that a particular decision arrived at would not automatically meet with the approval of the mob, would pass over a hogshead of good ale to Bowed Joseph to encourage him to appease his rowdy followers.

Sadly, returning from the Leith races in 1780, Bowed Joseph fell blind drunk from the top of a stage coach. He died immediately. Edinburgh had lost one of its most colourful characters.

THE ESCAPE OF JAMES HAY

One of the most remarkable escapes from the Tolbooth jail occurred in 1783. James Hay, a lad of eighteen, was the son of a stabler in the Grassmarket. In November of that year, he was a captive in the prison under sentence of death for robbery.

Some days before the execution young Hay was visited by his father who came to console his unhappy son. As night closed in visitors to the various felons were compelled to depart. Old Hay however invited the keeper of the inner key to partake in some of the liquor he had secreted about his person. The turnkey agreed with the unfortunate consequence that by ten o'clock — the hour for finally locking the gates — he was rather tipsy. Father Hay seeing that the bottle he had brought was now consumed suggested to the jailer that, as they were now just beginning to enjoy themselves, would it not be a good idea if another was procured. Hay in fact suggested that the gate keeper was the very man to perform this task.

The turnkey consented and staggered down the turnpike stair, neglecting to lock the inner door behind him. As had been plotted young James followed close behind. But just as the prisoner was about to spring into the street a free man, the outer warden closed the outer door, locking it securely. At that dread moment old Hay put his head to the great window of the hall and issued the widely known command of the time, 'Turn your hand', the cry which brought the outer turnkey to the door to unlock the external gate. Mechanically the man obeyed, the young offender sprang out and while the turnkey and old Hay jovially discussed the excellent quality of the rum, Hay fled at great speed down Beiths Wynd till he reached the high walls of Greyfriars churchyard. Scaling them with remarkable agility he entered the cemetery according to the prearranged plan. James had been provided with a key for the long unused mausoleum of Sir George Mackenzie. This gloomy domed edifice was a place full of terror to old and young alike, but especially to the boys of George Heriot's school. It was supposed to be haunted by the blood-red spirit of Mackenzie the persecutor. This is where Hay intended to hide.

On 24 November 1783 there appeared in the *Edinburgh Advertiser*:

ESCAPED FROM THE TOLBOOTH OF EDINBURGH
James Hay, indicted for highway robbery, aged about 18 years, by trade a glazier, 5 feet 10 inches high, slender made, pale complexion, long visage, brown hair cut short, pitted a little in the face with the small-pox, speaks slow with a haar in his tone, and has a mole on one of his cheeks. The magistrates offer a reward of Twenty Guineas to any person who will apprehend and secure the said James Hay, to be paid by the City Chamberlain, on the said James Hay being re-committed to the Tolbooth of the city.

But James Hay had been a 'Heriotier', brought up in the hospital-school which adjoins the ancient burial-ground; thus, he contrived to make known his plight to some of his erstwhile school-boy friends and besought them to assist him in his distress. It was impossible for his father to do so. A very clannish spirit existed amongst 'the Auld Heriotiers' in these days and not to give succour to an old comrade, no matter how undeserving, would have been deemed a crime of the foulest nature. Thus Hay's school chums supplied all his wants and needs from their own meals, carrying the food to the eerie hiding place at dead of night, risking severe punishment not to mention encounters with spectral beings in the graveyard.

This mission lasted for six weeks until the hue and cry abated and Hay left the tomb and escaped out of Edinburgh and beyond the reach of the law.

DEACON BRODIE

There can be few people in the English-speaking world who have not heard of Dr Jekyll and Mr Hyde. Very many fewer must be the number who know that the inspiration for Robert

Louis Stevenson's character was one of Old Edinburgh's most respected citizens, William Brodie, unparalleled cabinet-maker, Burgess and Guildbrother of Edinburgh, Deacon of the Incorporation of Wrights and Town Councillor.

William Brodie was born in 1741, one of 11 children of whom only three reached maturity. The well-to-do family lived in a fine town house mansion beyond the entrance to Brodie's Close (named after his father, Francis). Very little of Brodie's Close remains and nothing whatsoever of the home, it having been totally destroyed in order to build Victoria Street.

When his father died in 1782, William inherited £10,000 (a substantial amount!), house property around the High Street and his father's prosperous business. To all intents and purposes the deacon should have been well set up and able to live a very comfortable life. This, however, was not to be. For among his fatal weaknesses, Deacon Brodie was a gambler.

Deacon Brodie

Had this frailty been exposed to his social equals at 'The Cafe', Edinburgh's most aristocratic social club, it might have been dealt with. Unfortunately, Brodie sought out the dens of iniquity of which there were many in eighteenth century Edinburgh. James Clark was the owner of a disreputable tavern at the head of Fleshmarket Close. It was principally here that Brodie mixed with crooks and sharps. Brodie was regarded by his scoundrel drinking and gambling partners as their chief and one of the most enthusiastic partakers in that 'gentlemanly' vice, cock-fighting. He kept his own birds and lost large sums of money backing them.

Were all of this not enough, Brodie decided to compound his financial burdens by running three households. His legitimate family lived in Brodie's Close. His first mistress, Anne Grant, who bore him two girls and a boy, lived in Cant's Close. His second mistress, Jean Watt, who gave him two sons, dwelt in Libberton's Wynd. (It is interesting and presumably to some kind of credit to the ability of the man that neither of his mistresses knew of the other.)

Brodie's enthusiasm for plurality began long before his father's death — after all, it was surely a workload that could be borne only by a young man — and therefore gave him considerable financial burdens and responsibilities some years before he inherited his fortune. Means therefore had to be found to replenish his exhausted coffers.

Cheating his fellow citizens with loaded dice earned him only a few guineas. He had to go into the big time. Opportunity to do so was all around him. It was the habit of tradesmen of the day to hang the keys of their premises upon a nail at the back of the shop during business hours. Concealing a lump of putty in the palm of his hand, Deacon Brodie would drop in on these guileless merchants for a blether and as soon as they were distracted by a genuine customer, a quick impression of the key would be taken. The rest is obvious . . .

Midnight burglaries became a common feature of this honest town with Deacon Brodie as far above suspicion as the provost of the city or the minister of the High Kirk of St Giles.

In July 1786, there arrived in Edinburgh an Englishman called George Smith who was introduced to Deacon Brodie while lodging at the inn of the publican, Michael Henderson, in the Grassmarket. Smith had the double qualification of being both an established felon and a locksmith — two qualities from which Brodie felt he could substantially benefit. The two men — poles apart socially — became partners in crime.

In 1787, two additions were made to the band. On his arrival in Edinburgh, Smith had met in the same inn in the Grassmarket two petty villains, Andrew Ainslie and John Brown. It was clear that by this time Brodie was becoming ambitious. It appears that he had designs on the silver mace of Edinburgh University, then kept in the College library.

On the night of 29 October 1787, the four, 'having got access at the under gate, opened the under door leading to the library with a false key, which broke in the lock, and thereafter they broke open the door of the library with an iron crow and called away the College mace.' While, the next day, the mace was being removed from Scotland, Deacon Brodie as town councillor, displayed much official shock and horror at the effrontery of the outrage.

Many more and lucrative crimes were engineered and executed by the Brodie gang in the following year. But the biggest job was yet to come. The robbery of the Excise Office was intended to be the masterpiece which was to crown his career, free him from his accomplices and allow him to retire in comfort. The plan was long thought out and should have proved relatively easy to villains of such experience. None of this was to be, however. Just beyond the Netherbow and into the Canongate is a spacious enclosure named Chessel's Court. At the back of the court is a fine mansion which in the eighteenth century was the General Excise Office for Scotland. Housed in this building was much of the collected taxes and revenues of His Majesty's Scottish subjects. It goes without saying that they should have been lodged in a bank, but they were not.

It transpired that the Deacon had a relation in the excise business who had cause to come to Edinburgh and visit the office. Brodie decided that on this occasion he should accompany his cousin on his errand. Some days later, Brodie and George Smith returned, innocently seeking the cousin.

While the cashier was engaged in conversation with Brodie, Smith took an impression of the key which as usual was hanging on a hook behind the front door. After their departure Brodie drew a plan of the room, Smith made the false key and Ainslie studied the nightly patrols of the watchmen whose duty it was to guard the premises.

Armed to the teeth, the band — Brodie, Smith, Ainslie and Brown — set off on Wednesday, 5 March. If they were disturbed Brodie had instructed the men to behave like smugglers who were intent on recovering confiscated property. Entry was secured with reasonable ease on this freezing, pitch-black night. Events now adopted an element of farce. Although Ainslie was on guard he saw one figure rush into the excise office and a minute later two men left, some seconds separating their departure. Afraid that they were discovered, Ainslie blew the prearranged alarm whistle and departed hastily. He need not have bothered. No discovery of the robbery had been detected. The figure who entered and the second to leave was Mr Bonar, Deputy Solicitor of Excise who returned after work to remove some papers he had inadvertently left. Believing that some clerks would still be working at half-past eight he thought nothing of the door being unlocked. Indeed, he hoped it would be so. Shortly after entering the office, the deacon literally bumped into him. Although armed with a brace of pistols for any eventuality, Brodie decided against their use and felt retreat was the better part of valour on this occasion. In short, he fled.

Assuming this body to be legitimately connected with the excise office and still preoccupied with his desire for the papers, Mr Bonar ran upstairs, got what he wanted, ran down again and out the door.

Meanwhile, Smith and Brown, in another part of the building, continued their feverish search for the loot by the light of the deacon's dark-lantern. Ransacking everywhere likely to hold money, they found only £16 in a cashier's drawer. (Ironically, in a secret drawer beneath lay £600.) Shortly after, they too, left.

The next day the band met in the Cowgate to divide the spoils. This was the last time they met and the deacon was left in no uncertain terms that he was the villain in their failed enterprise.

At this point we must enter the mind of John Brown who had been plagued by temptation for some months. After a robbery at Inglis and Horner's silk mercer's shop at the Cross in the High Street towards the end of the previous year (which, incidentally, the Brodie band had done) a government reward of £150 was offered for information leading to the arrest and conviction of the perpetrators. More significantly, if this information was provided by an accomplice in the crime, the informant would be granted 'His Majesty's most gracious pardon.'

Thoroughly aggrieved, Mr Brown now intended to take advantage of this generous offer. On that same evening he went to call upon the Procurator Fiscal and poured out his all. Remarkably, no mention was made of the involvement of Deacon Brodie, presumably with a view to blackmailing him in the years to come.

The next day, Smith, his wife, their maidservant and Brown were lodged in the Tolbooth whereupon an attempt was made to visit the accursed felons by none other than Town Councillor Brodie. The keeper of the jail had orders to let no one enter and so the deacon, in his formal garb, was forced to depart.

Fearing the worst and his own skin, Deacon Brodie decided to continue his habit of fleeing. This time it was from the entire country. As investigations progressed, this proved to be a foolish and fatal mistake, for Smith and Ainslie denied all knowledge of the crime and still none had mentioned the name of Brodie.

It was only when they heard of the flight of their chief while they were ensconced in the Tolbooth that Mr Brown decided to make a further clean breast of the gang's misdoings. Immediately, a reward of £200 was placed on the head of 'William Brodie, a considerable House-Carpenter, and Burgess of the City of Edinburgh'.

The deacon skilfully managed to avoid the King's Messenger for Scotland all the way to London, so much so that the latter was forced to return to Edinburgh. With the aid of the lawyer, Brodie received papers and funds and a passage on one of the many Leith smacks which regularly sailed between the two capital cities. On Sunday, 23 March, Brodie embarked and joined the two other passengers — Mr and Mrs Geddes, tobacconists, from Mid-Calder. The *Endeavour* set sail the next day but soon ran aground at Tilbury Point in the Thames where it remained for a fortnight.

The tobacconist and his wife were unperturbed. This was an extension to their holiday. The fellow passenger, travelling under the name of 'Mr John Dixon' was less relaxed. When finally the *Endeavour* set sail, Mr Dixon presented sealed orders from the owners to the ship's captain instructing him to sail for Flanders and deposit the bearer at Ostend. Bad weather prevented this and the ship put into the fishing port of Flushing. From there Mr Dixon set off for Ostend in a hired skiff. Before taking his leave of his companions, Mr Dixon entrusted three letters to Mr Geddes to be delivered in Edinburgh. Of all the indiscretions which Deacon Brodie committed, this was the worst.

Finally, back in Leith, Mr Geddes purchased a local newspaper. Hardly had he begun to catch up on local news when his attention was caught by a public notice relating to Deacon Brodie. Instantly Geddes realised that Mr John Dixon and Deacon William Brodie were one and the same. He opened the letters which had been given to him for safe and speedy passage and discovered that their contents confirmed this. The Sheriff Officer was duly informed.

Within days he was traced to Amsterdam where he was captured and imprisoned in the Stadthouse. On 17 July he was returned to Edinburgh, examined, then committed to the Tolbooth.

The summer of 1788 found all four members of the band incarcerated in the same building awaiting trial. It appears that Brodie was not over-anxious about his future. In a letter to a magistrate friend whose visitation he requested, Brodie wrote, 'You'll be sure to find me at home, and all hours are equally convenient.'

Partner Brown had recently been granted a full pardon for all past crimes — one of which was murder — to enable him to be a witness for the prosecution. However, his would be the only damning testimony. At the beginning of August the Lord Advocate decided to accept Ainslie as king's evidence and proceed against Brodie and Smith only.

The trial, which began on 27 August, 1788, was a star-studded occasion. Principal among the judges was none other than Lord Braxfield himself, the Lord Justice Clerk. The Lord Advocate was Hay Campbell and the Solicitor General, Robert Dundas. Brodie was defended by the Dean of Faculty, the great Henry Erskine.

The trial was a spirited affair but even the brilliant Henry Erskine could muster little in the way of a meaningful defence. After 21 hours of continuous session, the jury was led away at six o'clock on Thursday, 28 August, to consider their verdict. When it arrived it was unanimous. Both were found guilty. The Lord Justice Clerk, Braxfield, pronounced sentence of death to take place on 1 October.

The prisoners were taken to await execution in the Iron

George Smith and Deacon Brodie

Room of the Tolbooth and there they were chained to the floor. Although his pleas to his influential friends to persuade the authorities to commute the sentence to transportation came to nothing, Brodie had a further plan in the pipeline. He conspired with the aid of a surgeon to 'cheat the wuddy'. On the morning of his death Brodie wrote to the provost praying that orders might be given to deliver the body to Mr Alexander Paterson, 'and by no means to remain in gaol'. The request was granted.

It is one of the great legends of old Edinburgh that Brodie was the first criminal to die by the newly introduced 'drop' and that he designed it. Enhancing our tale though this might, neither of these points is true.

His place of execution was on top of a single-storey building which projected from the Tolbooth. As usual for a good hanging, Town and Gown headed the multitude which filled the Lawnmarket. The deacon was dressed immaculately as he was led to the scaffold, bowing graciously to all as he went.

Mounting the platform with briskness and agility, he cast a professional eye over the apparatus. As the hangman was about to bind his arms he requested that they be left free. This was done. He untied his cravat, buttoned up his coat and waistcoat and helped the hangman to adjust the noose. Placing his left hand in his waistcoat, he drew the white cap over his head and dropped the handkerchief as the last signal. Then, horror! The halter was too short and needed adjustment. Brodie removed the cap and descended the platform to speak with some friends while the adjustment was made. A second attempt at hanging met with no greater success and a further interlude took place. At the third, success was achieved and the deacon dangled for all the city to see.

It is said in the tales of old Edinburgh that everything was going according to plan. Death was pronounced, the body cut down, placed in a cart and driven furiously round the back of the castle to the deacon's woodyard at the foot of Brodie's Close so that resuscitation might take place.

It has been said that the hangman had been bribed to tamper with the rope so as to give only a short fall and avoid dislocation of the vertebrae of the neck. This would make recovery medically possible.

According to another account, it is said that before leaving his cell for the last time, Brodie had been supplied with a small silver tube for insertion in his throat to prevent suffocation, and that wires had been carried down both his sides from head to foot to counteract the jerk of the fall.

Despite any or all of these precautions and in spite of the specially retained services of a French surgeon to bleed specific parts of his body in his own workshop after the hanging, Deacon Brodie was dead — or at least until the spirit of the man rose again as Dr Jekyll and Mr Hyde.

HOME IMPROVEMENTS

John Ballantyne, printer, of Trinity Grove was a very small man with a very large wife. In order to escape her omniscient presence he built himself a study with a door so narrow that his wife could not enter.

CHILD MURDER ON A SUNDAY AFTERNOON

Robert Irvine, a licentiate of the church, was tried for murder by the Baron-Baillie of Broughton. Irvine had been tutor to the two sons of a merchant who lived in a villa near the hamlet of Broughton. For reasons which need not be given here but involved the boys' knowledge of a liaison between Irvine and a serving wench, he conceived the idea of murdering the two lads. This he did on a Sunday afternoon, when he took the children for a walk on the green and gorse-covered slopes where York

Place and St Andrew Square now stand. Unfortunately for him — but fortunately for the service of justice — a gentleman strolling on the Castle Hill watched the whole horrific scene and raised the alarm.

The murderer was speedily caught red-handed, imprisoned in the Broughton Tolbooth, and on the following day was summarily tried and found guilty. The hands of the foul killer were cut off and he was hanged.

The village of old Broughton, 1852

SANGUINARY NEW YEAR RIOTS 1812

Riots were a common social activity in the Edinburgh of the early nineteenth century. During the New Year celebrations they were even more frequent.

On the night of 31 December and the morning of 1 January 1812, riots took place 'hitherto without example'. After 11 p.m. the principal streets were taken over by bands of rough young artisans and idlers from the lower parts of town. Armed with bludgeons they assaulted and for some time overcame the police. They knocked down many respectable citizens, robbing them of their watches, their money and their hats. Dugald Campbell, a policeman and James Campbell, a clerk, died of wounds after trying to deal with the rioters.

Two rewards of 100 guineas were offered for the discovery of the murderers. A number of youths were arrested. Three were tried at the High Court on 20 March 1812 for being 'art and part of the murders and of robbery'. Hugh McDonald, Hugh McIntosh and Neil Sutherland were hanged on 22 April on a gibbet and scaffold created opposite the Stamp Office Close in the High Street, where the policeman was killed. All three were under 18 years of age.

The executions created a huge sensation in the city. The whole event was designed as a dreadful example to the rioters. The proceedings were carefully planned, including a procession from the Tolbooth to the scaffold 'to impart solemnity to the awful scene'. It is said that such a gathering of people who came to witness the execution had never been seen on the streets of Edinburgh.

MINOR OFFENDERS

Only a few years before Robert Peel, the Home Secretary, began to radically reform the penal system of the country, two boys, Mair and Aitchison, both under 16 years of age, were sentenced to death for housebreaking at Coates Crescent. The year was 1818 and at that time there were still over two hundred offences which carried the death penalty. We are told that the youths cried most piteously when instructed to stand up to receive their sentences and fell down below the bar. They were subsequently supported by police officers in attendance when Lord Hermand passed the death sentence upon them.

Stamp Office Close

BACK TOO SOON

Banishment from the city or country was a frequently used punishment in times past. Sometimes it was indefinitely, but more often it was for a prescribed period. Woe betide anyone who returned sooner than permitted. In September 1807 Archibald Bigg, a resurrectionist who had been banished from Scotland was whipped through the streets of the capital for returning before his term had expired.

THE LONGEST HANGING

For a number of reasons, all of which now seem quite unsatisfactory, the Edinburgh Tolbooth Jail was demolished in 1817.

The first execution to take place in the area after the removal of the old prison was held on 30 December 1818 amidst the most horrible and inhumane circumstances imaginable.

Robert Johnstone, a wretched, simple young man of 20 was convicted and sentenced to death for armed robbery. Prior to the execution a scaffold was erected in front of the Signet Library in Parliament Square. The gibbet rested against the wall of St Giles.

At three o'clock in the afternoon the hangman performed his task. The lever was pulled, the trap-door opened, the drop took place. But the trap doors did not completely open. Johnstone's tip-toes touched the half-open trap door. The culprit remained alive, though insensible.

The Edinburgh mob was roused to fury at this display of incompetence and brutality. Enraged, they stormed the magistrates and City Guard off the platform. After their flight someone with a knife jumped on to the scaffold and cut the rope. He was followed by a lame man with a crutch and then a general rush ensued. The authorities were powerless. Johnstone was to some extent restored to his senses and carried off.

Furious, fearful and doubtless humiliated, Baillie Patterson, surrounded by a strong body of the Guard marched up the

Lawnmarket to the castle to summon military assistance. But halfway towards their destination they blundered into a section of the mob carrying the almost lifeless body of young Johnstone. The bearers quickly changed their course and turned down the High Street.

Opposite the police office they came up against a force of constables who had arrived on the scene. After a sharp encounter the crowd fled leaving their burden in the middle of the street. The constables carried Johnstone into the police office and awaited the arrival of a detachment of the 8th Regiment with loaded rifles brought down from the castle by the provost. A second force led by Major Graham followed shortly afterwards.

The streets were now cleared by the military and order was restored. Johnstone was visited by a surgeon and bled to ascertain whether or not he was alive. He was. The regiment of foot soldiers then surrounded the scaffold and, eight hours after the whole bloody affair started, Robert Johnstone was dragged out and finally hanged. Public disgust and outcry was great but apart from Johnstone the only other casualty of the event was the official who bungled the execution, John Foster, who was dismissed from his position by the magistrates of Edinburgh. The defectively constructed scaffold and all the accompanying paraphernalia were completely dismantled immediately afterwards.

MARY McKINNON

In March 1822, Mary McKinnon, innkeeper in South Bridge, was tried for the murder of William Mowat, clerk. It appears that the trial aroused great public interest. Throughout the trial Parliament Square was crowded.

She was charged with having, 'upon the evening of 8th February last, murdered the deceased by inflicting a mortal wound upon his left breast with a knife, of which he languished until the 20th of said month, when he expired.'

It was stated that Mowat and others had entered Mrs

McKinnon's public house. Being already intoxicated they conducted themselves riotously. McKinnon had not been in the house when the disturbance started and returned to find her house in great disorder with much of the furniture broken.

The gentlemen had been with some girls at the inn. On making to leave, the girls tried to dissuade them. One of the young ladies, McDonald, apparently used some force in trying to hold on to the revellers.

At that point, McKinnon entered the room and took a black sharpened table knife. A general riot erupted with blows being struck in all directions. She made a sweeping blow at the left side of Mowat with the knife pointed downwards. One of Mowat's friends found that he had been stabbed and placed him in a chair. Within minutes he was dead.

After much interrogation and cross-examining of the witnesses, the jury gave the verdict of guilty. His Lordship, the Justice Clerk, having put on the black cap pronounced the sentence that 'between the hours of 8 and 10 on the morning of 16 April next, the prisoner be hanged by the neck till dead, and her body be afterwards delivered to Dr Munro to be publicly dissected and anatomized.'

During her stay in prison it appears that McKinnon grew to accept her fate and even looked forward to her death as a relief from her suffering life. She waved to friends as she was paraded to the scaffold, still claiming that she was not guilty.

Over 20,000 people attended the execution in the High Street of Edinburgh.

BURKE AND HARE

Up the close and down the stair,
But and ben with Burke and Hare,
Burke's the butcher, Hare's the thief,
Knox the boy that buys the beef.

It was Voltaire who thought that mass murdering dated back to the first king, priest or hero. Certainly since that time there has been no shortage of that type of criminal who sees repetition as an obligatory part of his craft. Two notorious examples in Edinburgh's history of this black art were William Burke and William Hare.

William Burke was born in Tyrone in 1792. Although Roman Catholic his first occupation was as house-boy to the local Presbyterian minister. At the age of 26, having moved from one occupation to another — baker, weaver, batman, husband and father of three children — he decided to quit Ireland and move to Glasgow. There he became, like many of his countrymen, a navvy on the Union Canal. It was at this time he fell in with a doxy named Helen McDougal. Wandering the Lowlands the couple arrived in Edinburgh in 1819. Residing at the well-named Beggar's Hotel, they became pedlars of second-hand goods.

Around the same period Burke first encountered his future partner in crime, William Hare. Of like age, race and breeding we know nothing of William Hare until he arrived in Scotland. Like Burke, Hare became a navvy on the Union Canal in search of Eldorado. Moving to Edinburgh thereafter Hare moved into Mrs Log's Boarding House in Tanner's Close. Burke and Miss McDougal moved in to the same lodgings in 1826.

The two men are said to have been a lively contrast when they faced each other in court. To Burke's 'down-looking, sleazy look of a dog', his useless nose, his round unwrinkled cheeks, his short thick frame inept for any gait but a waddle, rose up in clear opposition to the fantastic Hare.

Hare was a 'spare wretch, gruesome and ghoulish'. He seemed much taller than his partner, all in lines instead of ill-drawn curves. His face was hollow. Two grey eyes set so far apart that he had difficulty in focusing them. He frightened those who saw him when his history was known, but in his former days gave only the impression of a *minus-habens*, not quite an idiot, but certainly a 'mad Irishman'. If Burke was a dog, an ill-bred country mongrel that on sight any shepherd would shoot, Hare's appearance had the insane levity of the wolf.

Of their women we contrast a virago with a drab. Helen McDougal was the sodden remains of a coarse beauty; morose and introspective. She was Presbyterian and feared hell by fits and starts.

After the death of Log, the landlord of Hare's boarding house, he took up with Log's wife, Margaret Laird. Mag Hare as she became known was lively and vivacious, a 'skinny, scranky, wizened jade', eager with her nails and her kisses. All drank to excess.

On 29 November 1827 Hare rushed into the back room occupied by Burke and announced the death of 'Old Donald'. A Highlander and army pensioner, old Donald was a good payer while in good health. But now the tenant was dead, owing £3 in rent. In rage and despair Hare talked wildly of throwing the body in the gutter. History then records that it was during this period of vitriolic ranting that Hare uttered the blasphemous words: 'the Body-Snatchers!'

The body-snatchers. To the rich it was a monstrous obscenity to be guarded against with forethought and precaution. To the poor it was the first horror of sickness and the last terror of death. The horror of being unburied by ghouls, carted to the dissection table and cut to pieces by the apprentice doctors was the dread of all.

By the beginning of the nineteenth century body-snatching was a speciality. It required patience, courage, training and resources. These were qualities quite lacking in Burke, the incompetent egotist. Although popular, mythical history would have it otherwise, Burke and Hare were not body-snatchers. They were murderers — a subtle difference.

That very afternoon Burke and Hare bought from the tanner in the close a sack of bark. When the coffin carpenter had finished and gone, the lid was prised up. The body was removed, the bark placed in the box and nailed up ready for pauper burial. After the town hearse removed the coffin, attention was once more turned to the body. One of the women was sent out to purchase a tea-chest. On her return, the body was placed therein.

After dark, they sold 'the thing' for £7 10s to Doctor Knox, 10 Surgeon's Square, the noted independent Professor of Anatomy. The deal in a second-hand soldier was thus completed.

Late that night on the spoils of their sale, the four begin to drink. Conversation speculated on the future. The women suggested that their men should go regularly into the business — hire a cart, buy two spades and mine cemeteries. But Burke was offended. His cowardice, his inertia, his fecklessness provided him with a thousand excuses. Violent quarrels broke out. Burke became exasperated by their determination. They were unaware of forces that were driving him; not into body-snatching but murder.

But now Hare had another problem. Another lodger, Joseph, the mumping miller, was dying of fever in the middle room. His death was not the problem. It was the tedious length of time he was taking to achieve it. All the time the rent bill was mounting. Then the fever began to scare away some of the other lodgers. Joseph was a hard dier. Something had to be done.

It was. When the fever had stopped they went to Joseph's room. He was alone. Burke took a pillow and placed it over

Surgeon's Square, Edinburgh

the nostrils of the body. When the dying Joseph began to kick and struggle Hare seized his legs. The murderers held fast and firm. The body became limp. A tea-chest was procured. A short journey to Surgeon's Square and £10 was placed in their hands. It was done — again.

But up to then Burke and Hare had been fortunate. The bodies had come to them. If their careers were to continue they would have to become hunters. They did.

Their first quarry was the old woman from Gilmerton, Abigail Simpson who was burked in February 1828. A seller of salt and camstone she was decoyed by Hare and his wife. Enticed into Tanner's Close the three began to drink. Too drunk to go home she was persuaded to stay the night. By the morning the old woman was vomiting. She was plied with more whisky and port until she fell asleep. Then, according to Burke in his confession, Hare laid hold of her mouth and nose while Burke held her hands and feet. Soon she was dead. After

Old houses in the West Port, near the haunts of Burke and Hare

dark the now familiar journey to Dr Knox's dissecting rooms was taken at the conclusion of which £10 was handed over by the good doctor.

Next was Mary Haldane, a faded prostitute. For her body we are told the fee was 'more than £10'. With experience, the two became utterly careless. They began to pluck right and left in the endlessly peopled crowd-stream that passed Tanner's Close as fancy or chance led them.

On 9 April 1828 the murder of Mary Paterson took place. This proved to be the first of the three cases on which Burke was charged and condemned.

Two young street walkers, Janet Brown and Mary Paterson, both good-looking and the latter in possession of a flawless body that was famous in the night-world of Edinburgh, were accosted by Burke in a grog-shop early one morning. After attempting to get them drunk, though Janet strongly resisted, Burke invited them home. Setting out on their journey Burke realised the journey to Tanner's Close was too far so the three headed for Gibb's Close in the Canongate. For there lived Constantine Burke, a scavenger in the service of the city police, and Burke's brother.

More drink was bought. Constantine went to work. Janet still resisted the liquor. Mary fell into a sound drunken stupor. Just when Burke was reaching a high point of exhilaration at the prospect of a double murder, in walked Helen McDougal and Constantine's wife. The former burst into a fury of jealousy. Burke smashed a glass on her head. Blood began to flow. Constantine's wife went off to search for Hare. Janet Brown, by now fearful of her own safety, speedily departed. Burke took Helen McDougal by the arm and flung her into the passage. Hare arrived. The rest was predictable. Mary Paterson soon found herself on Dr Knox's table. Even although the body was in fact recognised by a student, Dr Knox was so proud of it that he summoned an artist to enjoy and record the beauties of his latest subject.

A nameless Englishman ill with jaundice and two other stray women were killed and prepared in quick succession by stifling in the back room of the lodging house.

The daughter of Mary Haldane, a prostitute like her mother

and a little 'kenspeckled' (or touched), was invited by Hare to accompany him to Log's to hear news of her mother. There she was prepared, trussed and slaughtered.

Perhaps the cruellest murder was that which resulted from an accidental encounter. Burke would roam the streets for hours, like a tiger uncaged. In one of these prowls he came across an old drunkard. He was to be the next victim. At the very moment he had decided to take him back to his den, an old Irishwoman and her grandson approached. Catching his accent and his fine new clothes, the old woman asked for alms. Burke immediately let the old man drop. Almost without a second thought Burke led the destitute old woman and her deaf-mute grandson to the lodging house.

That night he throttled the grandson: the next morning he broke the boy's back, across his knee. Burke began to be consumed not by remorse, but by fear. What would the doctors have to say about this glut of double the explainable quantity? How were they to convey the double cargo without arousing suspicion? They decided to risk it.

Both bodies were stuffed in a herring barrel. A horse and cart were fetched.

But on entry into the Grassmarket, the horse stopped dead. It refused to move. Burke said afterwards, 'They thought the old horse had risen up in judgement against them.' Hare saved the night. A porter was summoned. He agreed to transport the barrel on his hurly to Surgeon's Square.

They were paid for their produce.

A blind joyous rage seized on them. They returned to the spot where they had left the horse in the charge of a beggar. Unresisting it was led away to a tannery nearby. There Burke slit its throat.

Burke's reaction to this incident was a depression. To cure it he and Helen McDougal went to stay with relatives near Falkirk. The holiday seemed to do Burke much good. He returned with new plans only to find that Hare had dared to kill on his own — a rag picker or basket woman. He had obtained £8 for the body and had kept it entirely for himself. A great quarrel ensued. Burke and McDougal moved out of the killing-shed at Log's and transported themselves to the house

The Grassmarket, from the West Port, 1825

of John Broggan, a carter, who was Helen's cousin. The house was situated on waste ground behind the West Port.

It was in this house that Helen's cousin Ann McDougal was murdered by Burke and Hare after she had accepted an invitation to come through from Falkirk to visit them in Edinburgh.

From then on, their friendship and partnership re-established, the number of murders is impossible to ascertain. This lack of evidence ceases with the disappearance of Daft Jamie and the murder of Widow Docherty or Campbell.

Daft Jamie was one of those inoffensive imbeciles for which by ancient and virtuous tradition the Scottish nation has always kept a respectful affection. Jamie was a well-known character in the Edinburgh streets. He was scrupulously clean, peaceable though very strong, affectionate to the world. His only fault was his liking for drink. This was his downfall. Enticed to Burke's lodgings at Broggan's, a horrible struggle ensued before they were able to take possession of the body. Burke received a terrible bite on the hand, which according to legend grew into a cancer.

During the last phase of the mass murders, any caution previously displayed by Burke and Hare was cast to the winds. No longer content to hide in the shadows of back rooms, they brought out their snares in public at full midday and shook them in the faces of the victims.

The case of the brisk little woman belongs to the last phase. Burke picked her up. He claimed relationship because she was named Docherty and brought her home. Two lodgers, honest beggars named Gray, were asked to leave the room. Gray and his wife went obediently to spend the night at Hare's now almost deserted lodging-house. When they returned to Broggan's the next morning they inquired about that queer little Mrs Docherty. To rest after the journey Mrs Gray settled herself near the bedfoot. Burke snapped at her, 'Keep out of there, out of the straw.'

Burke, Hare and his woman left the room leaving the Grays alone. Intrigued by their warning from Burke, the lady sneaked towards the forbidden, scratched the hay aside and saw the body of the brisk Mrs Docherty, naked, cold and blood-spotted. She screeched to her husband. The couple prepared to leave.

As they left through the only door of the house they crashed into Helen McDougal, the colour of the corpse they had just seen. Old Mr Gray explained their hasty departure. Helen sank to her knees and began to pray to them. She would give them £10 a week if they stayed quiet. But the Grays edged past her and made good their escape. They headed for the nearest police station.

Not till eight o'clock that night did Constable Ferguson arrive at the house. Finding the gang of four drinking and singing, the policeman eventually found his way to the bed.

There he discovered the rags, the spittle and the blood. Their end had come.

The trial of William Burke and Helen McDougal, in the Justiciary Court on 24 December 1828, caused a feverish excitement all over the country. There were 55 witnesses for the prosecution including William Hare and Mrs Log who had turned king's evidence. The Lord Advocate had little difficulty in proving the guilt of Burke who was sentenced to death by Lord Boyle. The charge against Helen McDougal was found 'not proven'.

On 28 January 1829 at the head of Liberton's Wynd, William Burke was hanged before a crowd of 20,000 people who stretched from the Bowhead to the Tron Kirk.

Forced to leave the city by the mob who demanded that a similar fate should befall him, William Hare had a miraculous escape from a burning limekiln in England into which he had been thrown by workmen who discovered his identity. Blind and hunted from place to place, he died in a miserable cellar in the East End of London.

The two women gradually vanished into obscurity but Dr Knox was slowest to disappear. After a few years of snarling obstination he too left Edinburgh, heading for a life of alcohol, squalor and destitution in London. Thus was the curtain rung

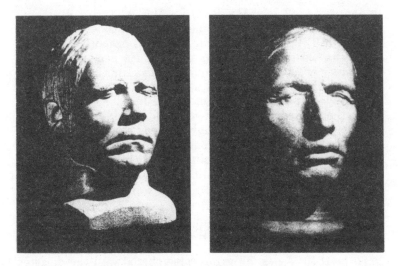

Life masks of Burke (left) and Hare

down on one of the darkest episodes in the whole of Edinburgh's history.

A NOTABLE DUEL

James Stuart of Dunearn was tried at the High Court for killing Sir Alexander Boswell of Auchinleck. The latter's death was the conclusion of a duel on 26 February 1822. Boswell had lampooned Mr Stuart in a Glasgow periodical called *The Sentinal*. The trial, which excited an unprecedented interest among all classes, resulted in the jury bringing in a verdict of not guilty.

STRANGE CONFESSION

In January 1832 John Howison, a pedlar, was tried, convicted and sentenced to death for the murder of a widow named Geddes, at Cramond. The night before his execution Howison made the most remarkable confession. He declared that he was guilty of six murders — four of the victims being children in Edinburgh. He stated that he committed the crimes while strongly under the influence of drink. Just for good measure he further stated that he had stolen four gold and a number of silver watches. But he strongly denied having murdered the widow. All this was beyond belief but said with the utmost composure. It made not the slightest bit of difference for he was hanged at the Calton Jail the next day.

HEAVE AWA

Born in 1843, Agnes Skirving remembered well the disaster which befell the part of the High Street where she and her family lived. Fortune's first blow struck Agnes when only newly into the world. A tipsy neighbour came in to see Agnes, the newborn baby, and while holding her on his knee upset the burning tobacco from his pipe into the infant's eye — extinguishing its light forever.

At the age of 18 Agnes lived with her parents and family above Paisley Close on the north side of the High Street. In the first week of 1861, she went to visit friends in Glasgow not realising that she would never see her family alive again. On Sunday 10 November a noise like thunder startled the sleeping High Street. The lofty tenement had collapsed in seconds and lay in a mass of debris around the street. Among the victims were all of poor Agnes's family. One of them, a sister, was saying goodnight to her fiancé who stood to bid farewell on the landing of the stair. For this young lady, the earth did indeed move. The crash came. She was hurled into eternity while he stood safe at the edge of the precipice.

Cramond

After the building collapsed, kettles could be seen on the holes of the fireplaces in the side walls still standing and a bird's cage with a living occupant still on its perch. The cage and bird were safely brought to ground.

Agnes used to tell how a grocer who occupied the ground floor and the cellars below the tenement and the pavement had cut a hole through the south wall of the building to give him room for a coffee mill. This could certainly have weakened the building. Also how a flesher going home later after selling off his last morsel to his Saturday night customers found that his door would not open when he turned the key. Forcing it with all his strength, he recognised that there was a risk in remaining there, so he quickly removed his wife and sleeping children minutes before the disaster.

The disaster is most widely known because of one particular incident. While the rescuers toiled to remove the bodies of the 35 victims and any survivors, a faint cry was heard from the rubble. A boy's voice cried 'Heave awa lads, I'm no deid yet,' words that now adorn the memorial bust of the boy on the keystone of the pend of Paisley's Close.

It is said that he lived well into the twentieth century. Agnes died at the grand age of almost 80 in Queensberry House, by that time a hospital.

JEAN BRASH

Around the middle of the nineteenth century one of the city's most noted thieves was Jean Brash. Promenading Princes Street one day in expensive furs she gave the 'glad eye' to a young dandy with more money than sense. Entering into conversation with the lady he soon found that a £5 note was missing from his pocket. A police constable was in the vicinity (as they say) at the time and Jean was charged with theft. She was searched on the spot, her pockets were turned out but no note was found. Protesting violently Jean was marched up to the Police Office in the High Street. Safely contained in the charge room she was searched more minutely by a female warder. The second search proved equally fruitless and allowed Jean to continue pleading her innocence.

By this stage the officer was beginning to doubt the dandy's story. After an hour Jean was set free. She returned to the corner of Princes Street and Castle Street and there caught sight of the policeman who had arrested her. Moving towards him, she stopped by his side and shook him effusively by the hand.

'What's your game now, Jean?' asked the policeman.

'I'll tell you where the £5 is if you promise not to blurt it to McLevy.* It would make a nice present to take home to your wife.'

Thrusting her nimble fingers into the cuff of the constable's coat, with flashing eyes she looked him straight in the face.

'Suppose you find the note in here after I'm gone. I'm sure you wouldn't know how it got there, would you?'

'No,' answered the constable excitedly.

'Then search your cuff!' cried Jean as she released hold of his arm. 'It's there — a bonny New Year's gift to take home to your wife!'

And before he had time to collect himself the woman had disappeared. The constable began to search but failed to find anything. Why? Because while pretending to put the £5 note in the cuff, she had actually abstracted the note which she had cunningly placed there when about to be marched off to the police station two hours before.

*'Jimmie' McLevy was Scotland's most noted detective in the nineteenth century. It is claimed that he solved over 3,000 cases during his 30-year career.

THE BLUE BELLS OF SCOTLAND

About 1850 a tenant in a flat in Coates Crescent went on a short holiday. On his return he found that burglars had been busy. Many valuables were missing. McLevy was called in to investigate. He got a list of the stolen goods — gold rings, earrings, brooches and a silver plate. The detective realised that it was going to be a difficult job. Most of the items could be melted down. The tenant realised that a small musical box was also missing. The instrument played *The Blue Bells of Scotland*.

Days of fruitless effort and investigation failed to produce a single clue. The great McLevy was ready to give up the chase. Sauntering down Blackfriars Wynd, he drew up at the door of a public house. Standing in the doorway he heard the tinkling sound of *The Blue Bells of Scotland*. The sound emanated from a small box at the bar. Entering the howff he ascertained from the landlady that the box had been left there accidentally by a man whom she went on to describe.

From the description McLevy spotted that it was one of his 'bairns' (a term used to describe the many Old Town petty felons on whom the detective kept a close eye). Immediately he went to the house where the 'bairn' lived. Eventually he

View of the Old Town from Princes Street

gained admission (for James McLevy's knock was well known to every one of the inmates). At a glance he unearthed the thieving gang. Two constables were summoned. The tenement flat was searched and within half an hour the whole of the stolen jewellery was recovered. The bairn and his companions were shortly afterwards tried and transported.

COFFINS ON ARTHUR'S SEAT

On a glorious summer afternoon in 1836 five young Edinburgh lads were chasing rabbits on Arthur's Seat. To make their hunt easier one of the boys had taken along his dog.

Out of sight for a moment they chased after the pet and found it scratching in the earth. The lads went to investigate and discovered not a rabbit hole but what looked like the entrance to a tiny cave. Scraping away the earth around the hole, one of the boys put his head inside to see how large it was — and quickly drew it out again. The hole was full of . . . coffins!

Plucking up the courage, all five entered. They counted 17 coffins, arranged in three tiers. Each one was only four inches long and, apart from the lids, made out of single pieces of wood. The lids were fixed on by two brass pins. The sides were decorated with tiny tin decorations.

Foolishly the boys began to throw the coffins at each other and some of them broke. Next day, they gave the rest to their teacher who was a member of the local archaeological society. The schoolmaster of course was curious to find out the nature of their contents. He prised one open and found a small figure inside, carved in perfect detail. Each of the other coffins contained the same bizarre contents.

Everyone in Edinburgh got to hear of the story. Endless discussions were held as to the origins of the coffins. Even *The Times* of London devoted a column to the story. But no solution was uncovered. Some of the coffins may still be seen in the Royal Museum of Scotland, Queen Street.

WILLIAM BENNISON

There has been no shortage of religious bigots in Edinburgh's illustrious past. One of the most notorious was 'Holy Willie Bennison'.

Bennison was not a Scot. He was born in Ireland and in 1838 married an Irish girl, Mary Mullen. Soon afterwards he deserted his wife and bigamously married Jean Hamilton from Paisley. However, he returned to Ireland to be with his first wife, Mary, and asked her to come with him to Scotland. She agreed and the couple left their native land.

However, soon after they set up home together, Mary Mullen died mysteriously. Bennison returned to his second wife, Jean and the couple moved into Steads Place, Leith Walk. They had a daughter and to all intents and purposes lived happily for several years. Bennison was a deeply religious man and the couple became enthusiastic and hard-working Methodists.

Bennison, however, began to waver from the straight and narrow. He started to court a young lady named Margaret Robertson. At this time Bennison's friends were told that Jean was unwell and generally suffering from a period of bad health. Mrs Bennison was in fact perfectly fit. But not for long.

In February 1850 Bennison bought some arsenic from a chemist's shop in the Kirkgate, Leith. He asked the chemist, as a favour, not to disclose the purchase to anyone. Within a fortnight Jean became violently ill. Bennison told her sister when she visited that a doctor should examine her but also said, 'It's no use, she is going home to glory.'

Ever prepared Bennison took a pair of black trousers to be mended. He said they would be needed if his wife died. That afternoon, 15 April 1850, she died. She was buried in Rosebank Cemetery. But hardly had the second Mrs Bennison passed away, than her wedding ring was taken from her finger by her husband who moved in with Margaret Robertson's family.

The finger of suspicion soon pointed to 'Holy Willie'. Firstly Jean's sister was more than a little curious why the grieving husband refused to allow a post-mortem. Secondly and more importantly the dog of a blind man who lived below the bigamist's house died after eating some of the porridge which the deceased had taken before she became ill. Bennison was arrested, tried and sentenced to be hanged for wife murder and bigamy. The execution was performed by Hangman Murdoch of Glasgow on 16 August 1850.

EUGENE MARIE CHANTRELLE

In 1866 a Frenchman, Eugene Marie Chantrelle, arrived in Edinburgh to begin a new life and to seek his fortune. He was 32 years old. Born in Nantes, he was the son of a wealthy and important family. A brilliant student, he distinguished himself at the Nantes Medical School.

However, at the age of 15 his father lost all his money, forcing Eugene to give up his studies and support himself. It appears that young Chantrelle managed to do this. He attended medical classes in Strasbourg and Paris but was unable to settle down to full-time study again. He never obtained his degree and his life became aimless and restless.

As a consequence of his involvement in French politics in 1851, when he was among those who objected to Louis Napoleon's bid for despotism, he found it advisable to quit France for at least the forseeable future. He first moved to the United States then on to England where he taught languages for four years. Finally he came to settle in Edinburgh. He continued to teach, taking pupils privately and joining the staffs of some of the city's private schools. Chantrelle became a great success and developed a considerable reputation as a schoolmaster. He wrote several French text-books. In addition to teaching French and German, he was also a fine tutor in both Latin and Greek. As well as being well educated, he was handsome and dressed elegantly in the dandified style of the mid-nineteenth century.

Thus it was that in 1867 Elizabeth Dyer, a pretty and headstrong girl at the Newington Academy fell in love with her language teacher. With the polished, almost affected,

George Street, looking towards St Andrew Square

charm of his nation, his cynical air, his dark moustache and side-whiskers, Eugene Chantrelle was to an impressionable, romantic schoolgirl a Byronic hero. Unfortunately Elizabeth and Chantrelle became lovers. As if that were not bad enough she soon discovered that she was going to have a child. Her family were outraged but to save her reputation reluctantly agreed to the couple marrying.

Elizabeth did everything she could to make the marriage happy and successful. She devoted herself to him. Chantrelle made a good income from teaching and the couple settled in a comfortable house at 81A George Street. However, within only a few weeks of their marriage, Chantrelle began to treat his wife abominably. He abused her continually and degraded her at every opportunity as if he felt she were to blame for their situation. He often threatened to take her life and once said he would give her 'poison which the faculty of Edinburgh could not detect'. He frequently struck her. Twice she had to seek the protection of the police. On one occasion he threatened her with a loaded pistol.

He was seldom at home. He was continually drunk and was openly and grossly unfaithful to her. Much of his time was spent in the many haunts of vice and depravity which were so easy to find beneath the veneer of Edinburgh's Victorian respectability.

In this way the marriage continued year after year. Elizabeth consulted a lawyer about the possibility of a divorce but knew that, as a woman, she and her children would face public disgrace and humiliation. By New Year's Day 1878 the Chantrelles had three children; a boy of ten, another of seven and a baby boy only two months old. Elizabeth was now a devoted mother as she had once been a devoted wife.

During the previous two years Chantrelle's treatment of his wife had improved. This was due to the court appearance when he was convicted of an assault on the servant girl in their home. But by the beginning of 1878 Elizabeth had much to cause her concern and unease. Chantrelle's life of debauchery was fiercely expensive. His teaching career was being neglected and by 1877 he was severely in debt.

In October of that year he made arrangements to have Elizabeth's life insured for the princely sum of £1,000, but only payable in the event of accidental death. His wife was unaware of the careful enquiries he had made defining 'accidental death'. Shortly before the New Year she told her mother, 'My life is insured now, and Mamma, you will see that my life will soon go after this insurance.'

On that New Year's Day Elizabeth, who was always in fine health, became sick. The servant girl, having been given the day off, returned in the evening to find her mistress in bed. The baby was beside her. Elizabeth told the servant that she had been ill but was better. The servant brought to her mistress some lemonade and peeled an orange, then retired for the night.

That night Chantrelle was the last to go to his room. The two older boys slept with him while the young baby needed such close attention. He went through to his wife's room and removed the baby from her side. The baby was given to the eldest child to look after on the pretext that their mother needed rest. He then returned to his wife's room where he stayed for some time before returning to his room.

The following morning the servant girl rose as normal at half-past six. As she prepared the morning tea the servant heard 'a moaning like a cat's'. When she heard it again she felt sure it came from her mistress's room. She entered and found Elizabeth Chantrelle moaning, but unconscious.

She rushed to rouse Chantrelle. It was unnecessary. He was already awake. The servant told him that his wife was ill. The two returned to Elizabeth's room where Chantrelle stood by her bedside for some minutes. Then suddenly he told the servant he could hear the baby crying and that she should go to attend to him. The girl did so but found the baby still fast asleep. Returning to the room once again she saw Chantrelle hastily move away from the window. He asked her if she smelt gas. The servant said she did not (later, however, she stated that she had).

Dr Carmichael, who lived nearby, was summoned. Chantrelle told the doctor that there had been a gas escape in the room. Examining Mme Chantrelle he found her unconscious and very pale and her breathing somewhat erratic. There was a smell of gas in the room although the supply had been shut off at the meter. Thus the doctor assumed that Elizabeth's condition had been caused by gas poisoning.

Coal-gas poisoning in the latter half of the nineteenth century was very rare. So Dr Carmichael sent a note to Dr Henry Littlejohn, the City Medical Officer who was an expert toxicologist. This invitation to the eminent doctor was most fortuitous, for it transpired that Dr Littlejohn knew of the Chantrelles. Some time before, Elizabeth had consulted him when her husband's behaviour was such that she felt he must have reached a state of insanity. So despite his agreement that this was a case of coal-gas poisoning he knew the state of the Chantrelles' marriage and was immediately suspicious. Instantly he had Elizabeth removed to the Royal Infirmary.

Early that afternoon Dr Maclean, Professor of Medical Jurisprudence examined Elizabeth Chantrelle. To him there was no indication of coal-gas poisoning. It was clearly a case of narcotic poisoning. He believed the substances used were either opium or morphia. At four o'clock that afternoon Elizabeth Chantrelle died.

A post-mortem was held the following day. No trace of coal-gas was found in the body. But neither were there traces of any narcotics. It was possible that traces of drugs could have disappeared. That would not have been the case with coal-gas.

However, it was not only her body that was examined. On Mme Chantrelle's nightdress and bedclothes stains were discovered which unmistakably contained traces of opium. Amazingly, a quantity of opium was discovered in the medicine chest in Chantrelle's own room. The gas had escaped from a long disused pipe, a portion of which had been freshly broken off.

On 5 January, immediately after his wife's funeral, at which he displayed intense grief, Eugene Chantrelle was arrested. His trial for murder lasted for four days in May 1878. At the end of it he was found 'Guilty of murder as libelled' and sentenced to death. He protested his innocence to the end. It did him no good.

On the eve of his execution Chantrelle showed something of his old style. He asked the Governor of the Calton Jail to provide him with three bottles of champagne and a whore for the night.

Although nothing could be seen, a large crowd gathered on Calton Hill early on the bright sunlit morning of 31 May 1878. For on that day Eugene Chantrelle was hanged.

THE MIRACULOUS FALL

In 1937 a young man whose name never seems to have been disclosed fell 106 feet from Thomas Telford's Dean Bridge. This bridge stands over the Water of Leith and Dean Valley. The young man was seen to fall from the parapet of the bridge. A policeman who seriously believed the man to be dead or fatally injured ran down to the river's edge after summoning

The Dean Bridge

an ambulance. The young man stood up in the river into which he had fallen, walked out practically unaided and stepped into the waiting ambulance.

He was driven hastily to the Royal Infirmary. The astonished doctors, after keen examination could find no injuries. He was however detained for observation and then released.

The reader who is unable to conjure up a picture of this incident would do well to make a visit to the Dean Bridge to appreciate the miraculous nature of the fall. (No attempt should be made to reconstruct the event without the aid of a parachute.)

SINISTER STORIES
OF
OLD EDINBURGH

THE KING, THE STAG AND THE CROSS

Not all phantoms and apparitions which have appeared in the city's history have taken human form. One of the most dramatic encounters took place on a Sunday in 1128. Because it involved the king and because the incident took on a profoundly religious significance, the tale has become as much myth as legend.

David I, son of Malcolm Canmore and Queen Margaret (who was later promoted to Saint), was determined to go out hunting on the slopes of Arthur's Seat within the Royal Park. Against all the advice of his leading clerics to do such a thing on the Sabbath, the king set off from the royal residence.

Interior of Holyrood Abbey Church

A good horseman and doubtless galloping at some pace, the king was suddenly attacked by a wondrous stag, 'the farest hart that ever was sene afore with leavand creatour.' King David was thrown to the ground and was about to be crushed to death by the massive antlers of this supernatural animal. The king reached up to its antlers to try to save himself and was stunned to see a cross appear in the middle of these fearsome horns. Being a monarch of deep religious conviction (though apparently not deep enough to dissuade him from hunting on a Sunday) the king grabbed hold of this cross. As he grasped it tightly, the stag vanished.

This incident affected King David so profoundly that he pledged himself to build an Abbey of the Holy Rood near where the 'miracle' took place. He kept his promise.

SIR RICHARD LAWSON

The most significant event of 1513 in the history of Edinburgh and Scotland was the disastrous battle of Flodden. A number of supernatural happenings took place at this time, all understood by everyone except the king as warnings against engaging the English in battle.

While King James was at prayer in the Abbey of Holyrood, a fiendish cry was heard at midnight at the Mercat Cross. The cry was uttered by Plotcok, alias Pluto — in other words the devil. Standing at the Mercat Cross with two of his diabolical disciples at his side, Satan proceeded to read out a list of names of people who were to appear before him in the Underworld within 40 days, that is, people who were going to die and unquestionably go to Hell.

This summons was heard by Sir Richard Lawson who was making his way home to the High Street beyond the Mercat Cross. Fear gripped Sir Richard as he heard the satanic roll call. The list began with James, the King of Scots himself. After the sovereign's name the devil summoned individually the dukes, earls, lords, barons, gentlemen and sundry burgesses who were also commanded to attend the devil's presence within the said time.

Towards the end of this list Sir Richard Lawson heard his own name being called. Lawson ' . . . ganging in his gallery stair, fornent the Cross . . . he cried for his servant to bring him his purse, took out a crown and cast it down the stairs from the gallery saying, "I for my part, appeal from your summons and judgement and take me to the mercy of my God!"'

Shortly afterwards the Scottish army led by King James IV went off to fight the English at the Battle of Flodden. It is said that it was the one time in Scotland's history when we had greater numbers than they had and we lost — wholeheartedly we lost!

And who died in that battle? James, the King of Scots, and every one of the dukes, earls, lords, barons and sundry burgesses whose names were called out by the devil to Sir Richard Lawson — all, except Sir Richard Lawson. The only man who returned to tell the tale; the only man who had appealed to God to escape the judgement of the devil.

WITCHES AT THE HIGH COURT

Towards the end of January, 1590, the witches of North Berwick were put on trial at the High Court in Edinburgh. Their crime was against no less a person than James VI, King of Scots. It was said that during the sea voyage from Scotland to Denmark which the king was making to meet and marry his future queen, the witches tried to cause the entire destruction of the king's fleet. They connived to whip up a furious hurricane which would bring an end to James and his entourage. Able though the witches undoubtedly were, they were aided by the devil who appeared to them wearing 'a black goon with a black hat on his head' and with 'claws on his hands and feet like a griffon'. Their preparations were also enhanced by baptising a black cat which was flung into the sea at Leith Pier. However, James succeeded in reaching Denmark, marrying Anne and went on to survive the return journey. The witches, however, only just survived their trial. They were burned at the stake shortly after.

DR JOHN FIAN — A NOTABLE SORCEROR

One of the highlights of the winter of 1591 in Edinburgh was the termination of 'the damnable life of Doctor Fian, a notable sorceror'. We do not know much of the early life of Dr Fian (alias John Cunningham). He first appears in history as a schoolmaster at Prestonpans, a few miles to the east of the capital. However, it seems that the rigours of the blackboard were to be replaced by those of the black arts. The devil was to become his master and Dr Fian, his clerk and registrar of witches.

Under his tutelage were Agnes Sampson, a midwife, Barbara Napier, the wife of a citizen of Edinburgh, and Euphame McCalyean, a lady of rank, daughter of a deceased judge of the Court of Session.

Dr Fian confessed to first being involved in witchcraft in order to obtain the love of a woman. We are told that in the same neighbourhood there was a rival for the affections of this young woman. So, 'by means of . . . sorcery, witchcraft and devilish practices' he caused the gentleman to turn quite mad.

At this point in the story a new character appears on the scene – none other than King James VI. The king's interest in witchcraft, demonology and the supernatural are well known. His Majesty became particularly involved in the prosecution of Dr Fian, so much so that after the initial tortures to obtain this first confession, Dr Fian was taken before the king for questioning.

The king was in for a rare treat for, on 23 December, 1590, the temporarily mad victim of Dr Fian was called as a witness. Hardly had he entered the king's chamber where Fian's trial was being held than he reverted to a state of madness and lunacy which lasted a full hour. Bounding into the air till his head hit the ceiling, then crouching as low as his contorted body would allow, his actions became too violent for the many attendant persons to restrain him. Greatly impressed as His Majesty was by all this maniacal activity he allowed the gentleman's fury to continue till exhaustion set in. After an hour the man returned to his senses and when questioned by the king as to what he remembered replied that he was aware only of being in a sound sleep.

The doctor also confessed that believing his favours towards the young woman would come to nothing he employed one of his young scholars, a brother of the lady, to obtain three strands of her hair. A wonderful piece of irony now ensued. The young boy's actions aroused suspicion in his mother who coincidentally just happened to be a witch. Keen to know what her son was up to she thrashed him relentlessly 'with sundrie stripes' until he told her.

The reader may find what is now written rather difficult to swallow but not nearly as hard as did Dr Fian. The mother-witch took from her son the piece of folded paper into which the hairs were to be placed and went into a field where stood a heifer which had never been able to calf. With a pair of shears she cut off three hairs from the udder of the cow and wrapped them in the same paper. The boy was sent off to fulfil his task.

The doctor went to the nearby church and performed some diabolical incantation over the hairs. Opening the door of the church to await his beloved, the doctor beheld the heifer standing there. Quite unnatural in its countenence, it entered the church following the fearful doctor wherever he went 'leaping and dancing upon him'. Love was undoubtedly in the air. A small group of local residents looked on amazed as Dr Fian finally managed to escape.

Before and between sessions of his trial Dr Fian was subjected to various forms of torture to help the proceedings move smoothly along. 'Thrawing his head with a rope' achieved nothing. Ordinary persuasion, not surprisingly achieved nothing. However three strokes of the 'bootes', 'the most severe and cruell paine in the world', had more effect. But after the 'bootes' was employed on this occasion and it seemed that the doctor was likely to be more co-operative, it appeared that he was unable to speak. Close investigation revealed two sharp iron pins concealed under his tongue which because of the torture were now thrust up into his head. These pins, which were believed to be a devilish charm, were removed and the prisoner was once more brought before the king.

Here he confessed to frequent conferences with the devil, attending various meetings of the witches in his charge at which the devil was in attendance, going to Prestonpans one night with his ladies and by their incantations causing a ship to sink and chasing a cat in order to fling it into the sea as a means of causing much maritime destruction.

After this examination Fian was placed in a separate cell of the Tolbooth Jail. Here he quickly 'came to a state of penitence'. He renounced the devil and all his conjuring, witchcraft, enchantment and sorcery. He accepted God and vowed to lead the life of a Christian.

The following day, however, he told his jailors of the vision he had had that night. Satan had appeared to him. The devil, realising that he was losing a disciple, said to him 'Ere thou die, thou shall be mine,' at which point Satan broke his white wand in two and vanished.

Remaining with God that day, Dr Fian nevertheless contrived to steal the key from his keeper and escaped, fleeing the city. The king was informed and instructed that he be apprehended, 'by means of hot and harde pursuit'. The doctor was caught.

The affairs of state being apparently none too overwhelming at this time, Dr Fian was brought before the king. James VI was concerned that a new pact with the Prince of Darkness had been entered into. The monarch was correct. Dr Fian now denied all that he had confessed to, even although it was scribed and subscribed by him.

There was nothing for it. Back to the torture chamber he went. His body was searched for new marks of the devil. None was found. One by one his finger nails were wrenched out with pincers; needles were then thrust their full length into each finger. Once more he was placed in the 'bootes' for so long that his legs were beaten together and crushed, his bones and flesh bruised so that 'the blood and marrow spouted forth in great abundance'. He resisted all.

It was clear to King James and all those in attendance that the devil had truly re-entered his heart. There was nothing else for it. He was condemned to death and burned at the stake.

AULD CLOOTIE

The devil — a frequent visitor to the city — has rejoiced in many names, none more Scottish than the nomenclature used at the end of the sixteenth century: Auld Clootie. It was as this that he most disastrously descended one dark afternoon exactly 400 years ago. Sir Lewis Bellenden, a Lord of Session and superior of the Barony of Broughton invited the devil in all his satanic majesty to visit the backyard of his house in the Canongate. To aid him in his supernatural exercises Sir Lewis had employed Richard Graham, 'a notorious trafficker in the darker arts'.

The appeal to Auld Clootie was so successful that as a consequence of the fiendish experience the judge died only a few days later.

AGNES SAMPSON

During the reign of James VI when much demonic activity was present in the capital, Agnes Sampson was charged on 53 counts of sorcery. A grave, matron-like woman, she was able to cure the sick, both animal and human, and with the help of her familiar, the devil, she could prophesy the future.

Her confession was not achieved unaided. Tortured by the twisted rope round her head which apparently she endured for an hour, she finally confessed. On one occasion she visited a sick boy in Prestonpans and while uttering incantations throughout, she 'graipet him' — felt him over. Within minutes he was healed.

While attending some sick cattle she moved between them in their stalls, stroked their backs and bellies, all the while chanting the *Ave Maria* over them. They recovered. Much more exciting was the cure of Robert Kerse. He had been heavily tormented by witchcraft and disease which had been laid on him by a warlock. She took his sickness on herself and became tormented throughout that night. So much so that in a state of raving madness she threw herself out into the close. There she transferred the torment to Alexander Douglas who over the next few days wasted away and died. Robert Kerse was, we are told, 'made hale'.

Not so successful was her treatment of Lady Edmeston. The old lady lay sick and was attended by Agnes. Before she left she informed the group of gentlewomen who were there that she would know by that evening if Lady Edmeston would recover. She charged them to meet her in the garden after supper between six and seven o'clock. Agnes then departed and went to spend some time in prayer in the garden of the house. She summoned the devil, whom she called Elva to come and speak to her. Right on cue, he bounded over the wall in the form of a large hound. Agnes was scared. She commanded the devil to come no nearer.

History now records the actual conversation which took place between Agnes and Satan. Asked whether the lady live or not, Satan replied, 'Her days are gone.'

'Give the gentlewoman her daughters,' he said, and then asked 'Where are they?'

'The gentlewomen said that they were to be here,' Agnes answered.

Satan announced, 'One of them shall be in great peril. I shall have one of them.'

Agnes, obviously braver by this time, replied, 'It shall not be so.'

At this juncture in the dialogue the devil left yowling, but remained at hand hiding in the well. When Lady Edmeston's daughters appeared the dog jumped out of the wall and stood before them staring demonically at each one. Lady Torsonce, one of the daughters, ran to the well completely against her will. Undoubtedly the devil intended to drown her but Agnes and the other daughters ran to her rescue. Foiled by this challenge, the dog disappeared with a yowl that could have raised the dead.

124

Agnes Sampson met the devil again. This time outside Edinburgh — in North Berwick church. The North Berwick witches as we have read are famous, particularly because of their attempt to prevent King James VI bringing his new queen, Anne, across the seas from Denmark. The attempt of course failed.

Agnes was one of those witches. Appearing one night from the pulpit in the church, 'like one meikle black man' the devil took a roll call of his disciples. Thereafter he commanded them to open the graves — two inside the church and two in the graveyard. This they did and at his instruction began to remove from the bodies the joints of their fingers, toes and knees and passed them out evenly amongst the group. Then 'to do evil withal'.

The devil thereafter ordered them to perform an act of homage to his greatness. Heaving his demonic buttocks over the side of the pulpit the devil required the company of witches to kiss this area of his satanic anatomy as a sign of their loyalty and obedience.

Agnes was undoubtedly one of the most versatile of Scottish witches to be convicted in Edinburgh. During her trial in Holyrood Palace, King James referred to her as an 'extreme lyar'. He apparently caused the witch great offence. So proud that she was at all times telling the truth, 'she declared unto him the very words which passed between the King's Majesty and his Queen at Upslo in Norway, the first night of marriage, with their answer each to other.' This seemed to have the desired effect because the king announced that all the devils in Hell could not have known that.

Impressed though he was, the king judged that Agnes should be taken to the Castle Hill, strangled at the stake and her body burned to ashes.

DYING IN DESPAIR

In the minutes of the Scottish Privy Council for 1 December 1608, it was reported that 'the Earl of Mar declared to the council that some women were taken in Broughton as

Edinburgh Castle and Castle Hill

witches, and being put to an assize, and convicted, albeit they persevered constant their denial to the end, yet they were burned quick, in such a cruel manner that some died in despair . . . ' (Typical civil service understatement.)

AGNES FYNNIE: INDUSTRIOUS WITCH

Edinburgh, in its long history, has had no shortage of witches. One of the most celebrated and judging by what follows, most active, was Agnes Fynnie who lived at the Potter Row Port of the city. She was prosecuted for witchcraft in 1644, with 20 charges made against her. Collectively, they read like a handbook on how to be a successful sorceress.

On one occasion while running to his house, the young son

of Mr William Fairlie passed by Agnes and hailed her 'Agnes Winnie', an impromptu nickname he was soon to regret. Within 24 hours young Fairlie had lost the power of his left side, become bedridden with 'so incurable a disease' and literally began to fade away. He died a week later from what the physicians described as the 'supernatural'.

To a neighbour, Beatrix Nisbet, Agnes gave a most 'fearful disease' so that she lost her powers of speech. Worse was to befall Janet Grinton who sold two herrings which Agnes considered were not fresh. Agnes returned the fish, requested the return of the 8-penny purchase price (whether or not she got her money back we do not know) and informed Janet that she would never eat another thing in this world. Sure enough the fishwife died without any further food or drink passing her lips.

Mr John Buchannan's son was suffering from the palsy. Agnes visited the sick child and after a few moments suggested that the parents go to another room and pray for the health of their son. When they returned they found their son so ill that he was unable to move any part of his body. To their further horror they discovered on his right buttock a wound as wide as the palm of a hand, as if a large chunk of meat had been hacked out of it. As a result of her 'devilrie', it was said the child died within a week.

Agnes was not yet finished with this family. The child's mother Bessie Currie and Agnes got into some kind of heated dispute over the changing of a sixpence. Agnes, who was obviously getting the worse of the deal, threatened to summon the devil to come and take a bite out of Mrs Currie. It seems that at this point Mr Buchannan appeared on the scene and taking his wife's side in the dispute incurred Agnes's wrath. He called her a witch and threatened to launch her over the staircase. That night Mr Buchannan became violently ill, burned all night with a fever, but seemed to recover the next day. John finally got the upper hand in this dispute. Returning to see her the next day, he threatened to tell the whole town how ill Agnes had made him if she did not lift her evil from his body. In an instant he became better . . .

But not for long. Some time later, John, who it would seem

never knew when to quit, did battle once more with the witch. Agnes apparently refused to give Bessie Currie a 12-penny cake on credit. John uttered some words to Agnes which offended her, whereupon she insisted that he vacate the premises and, as his birth had no doubt been caused by a witch, so too would his death. Immediately after 'he contracted a long and grievous sickness, whereof he was lyke to melt away in sweiting.'

Euphame Kincaid fared better. Her daughter did not. While Agnes and Euphame were at loggerheads one day Agnes had recourse to call the lady a drunkard, to which Euphame responded by calling her opponent a witch. Agnes replied that if this were so Mrs Kincaid and her family had better watch out. Accordingly a great wooden beam fell on Euphame's daughter's leg while she was playing near Agnes's house, and smashed it to pulp.

Although Agnes Fynnie did not allow easy terms to Bessie Currie for her 12-penny cake, it seems she did give credit to Isobell Atcheson. However, when the time came to settle the account and the ladies disagreed over the amount due, Agnes once more summoned the devil to ride about Mrs Atcheson and her family and wreak havoc upon them. Predictably the next day the unfortunate woman fell from her horse and broke her leg.

As we have seen, Agnes was a lady well able to defend herself against slanderous attack. She was just as capable of protecting her family.

Robert Wat, deacon of cordiners (shoemakers) had the lack of foresight to fine Agnes's son-in-law, Robert Purse, for riotous behaviour. Outraged Agnes went to where the shoemakers were meeting and whacked Mr Wat over the head with her cap. Not a particularly diabolical act but from that moment Robert Wat's business went into a rapid decline. Much time passed. One afternoon Mr Wat was spending some time with Agnes's grandson when the lady arrived unexpectedly. Reminding him of the blow to his head Agnes pointed out that his business would continue to plunge towards bankruptcy until he made amends to her and her son-in-law. Speedily the fine was returned and apologies came forth. Within a month Robert Wat returned to his former prosperity.

It appears from the evidence we read that Agnes Fynnie ran some kind of general store to which amazingly people took their custom. One such person was Christian Harlow who ordered and received delivery of some salt. Taking her life in her hands she returned the salt with the message that the amount was too small for the sum paid. Here we have an example of Agnes's true abilities. For without even seeing her, Christian fell grievously ill. Agnes was summoned to the death bed and, we are told, lifted the spell. Christian Harlow recovered.

Payment of bills was obviously a sore point with Agnes. Christian Sympson owed Agnes money. When the day of reckoning arrived Christian asked for a further eight days delay. Agnes flew into a rage and stated that she should have a sore heart if the account was not paid by that time. It wasn't paid, and the day after Christian Sympson's husband broke his leg.

Simply for calling Agnes a witch, John Robieson was flung into a fever.

Because he discorded with Agnes's daughter, John Cockburne was terrified during the night by the appearance of Agnes in his bedroom — having entered with doors and windows bolted securely.

Ruin was brought upon William Smith so that he would never be able to reclaim some clothes he had pawned at Agnes's shop.

For what reason we do not know, but Janet Walker received 'a grievous sickness' from Agnes while she was in an advanced state of pregnancy. Only when Agnes was summoned and the mother-to-be's health was begged for by her sister did Janet recover.

Margaret Williamsone and Agnes fell into 'a contraversie'. During this disagreement Agnes wished for the devil to 'blow hir blind'. Soon after, she became ill and, guess what, turned blind.

Agnes's daughter was not one for simply 'discording' with men, she also enjoyed a good brawl. Agnes was branded a witch for not only turning Andrew Wilson (the other party in the brawl) completely mad, but also for making him sane again.

Finally Agnes Fynnie was accused of having consulted and consorted with the devil for 28 years and for boasting that she was a 'rank' witch, that is a grand, proud and noble witch. She was condemned to be 'worried' (strangled) at the stake and then burned to ashes.

WIZARD OF THE WEST BOW

Thomas Weir was born at Kirkton near Carluke in Clydesdale in 1599. His father, Thomas Weir of Kirkton, was a man noted for his treachery. His mother was, according to his sister, Jean, a sorceress of some repute who bore the witch-mark on her forehead which enabled her to tell 'the secretest thing that any of the family could do, though done at a great distance.'

We know nothing of Thomas Weir's childhood, which is probably just as well, and first hear of him as a lieutenant in the Puritan army in 1641. More importantly, he became an officer in the Covenanting army during the Marquess of Montrose's campaign.

In 1649, the year King Charles I finally lost his head, Major Weir retired from active service. He settled in Edinburgh and accepted the esteemed post of Captain of the City Guard. Throughout its history the City Guard had been as much a source of amusement as of dread. This venerable body of armed men had its origins in the years following the defeat of the Scots at Flodden in 1513. Legend, however, places some of the City Guard in Jerusalem at the Crucifixion and during the commotion which ensued, the said respectable Edinburgh citizens carried off from the Temple an original portrait of none other than King Solomon. By the end of the eighteenth century their prestige had declined and they became known as 'that black banditti'. In 1817 they were finally disbanded.

When first in Edinburgh, Major Weir boarded in the Cowgate with the widow Grissald Whitford. One of his fellow lodgers was the preacher and assassin, Mr James Mitchell, who was hanged in 1678 for the attempted murder of Archbishop Sharp in the High Street of Edinburgh.

As Captain of the Guard, as a relentless pursuer of Royalists, as a former leader of the Puritan army and as a violent opposer of bishops in Scottish churches, Major Weir received the ultimate accolade from the people of Edinburgh — Major Weir became a worthy 'whom God had raised up to support the Cause.'

It was as one of Edinburgh's most notable 'worthies' that Major Weir moved from the Cowgate to the West Bow. This area of old Edinburgh formed part of the zig-zag route which steeply descended from the castle to the Grassmarket. The improvers of the city destroyed this thoroughfare towards the end of the nineteenth century so that nothing but the name remains. The Bow had during the seventeenth century long been the domain of the white- or tin-smiths who were a particularly godly group of people. So fiercely religious were they that they were known as the Bowhead Saints. They would have rejoiced when Major Weir arrived to live amongst them.

After his retiral from his post as Captain of the City Guard two years after it was bestowed upon him, Major Weir had more time to devote to spiritual matters. Truly, Major Weir seemed a Godsend. His imposing personality, his claims of phenomenal sanctity, his astounding memory which allowed him to quote the scriptures accurately and at length and his miraculous gift for leading public prayer all assured his pre-eminence among the Bowhead Saints. Meeting in their homes as they did, no 'household conventicle' was complete without his splendid whining and sighing.

Regarded as more angel than man, Angelical Thomas would never be seen 'in any holy duty without his Rod in his hand.' The full extent of the major's dependence upon his famous staff was not fully understood till later.

Major Weir did not live alone in the West Bow. His sister Jean, or Grizel as she was referred to by some contemporary authorities, lived there also and kept house. Much of what we are soon to read of Major Weir, and even more that cannot be written, included his sister Jean.

Many of us have Jekyll and Hyde qualities in our characters. It is only the Major Weirs of this world — or the next — that have three sides. Of Weir the saint we have read; of Weir the sinner we shall not, though we may care to take some time to ponder the infinite examples of human depravity and debauchery of which man is capable and assure ourselves that Major Weir would be involved in many of them. It is worth considering not the contradiction between Angelical Thomas and Weir the sinner, but the convenience of the two roles. To his benefit alone they complemented each other perfectly.

This was a man's world and if women were not good wives, mothers and workhands, they were witches and harlots — or so it was assumed. One instance of this was when a young lady, having observed what Major Weir was doing in a field in New Mills in the County of Lanark, complained to the minister, Mr John Nave. The minister had Major Weir brought to the magistrates but in the absence of further proof of his agricultural pastimes, the damsel was 'whipped through the town by the hand of the common hangman, as a slanderer of such an eminent Holy Man.' Any others who had tales to tell invariably kept them to themselves!

The end came with startling and dramatic suddenness. In the early spring of 1670 one of the great and gloomy gatherings of the faithful assembled in their high priest's house in the West Bow. Major Weir was by this time in the seventy-second year of his treble life. He was a weak and failing man, long worn down by vice and perversion. We do not know why but on this occasion instead of the usual 'Enthusiastical phrases, Extasies and Raptures' he rose to pour out a full confession of his life. Stunned and amazed, the brethren sat as if smitten by a thunderbolt from God. Had our gutter press been around these centuries ago they would have offered millions for the story.

'Before God,' he cried, 'I have not told you the hundredth part of that I can say more, and that I am guilty of.' But enough was enough. 'With all possible care and industry' the faithful made plans to keep this astounding scandal within the bosom of the elect. It must be made known that the saint had been seized with a violent illness which made him rant and rave. The reputation of the Bowhead Saints had to be preserved. For several months they were successful and they actually managed to control their own religious sect for the first time in a generation. However, the devil was not to be deprived

Major Weir's Land — the West Bow

of his due. One of the city's ministers, possibly Master John Sinclaire, unveiled all before the Lord Provost, Sir Andrew Ramsay, who the following year became a Senator of the College of Justice.

Considering the case deeply, the Lord Provost concluded that the case merited medical rather than criminal treatment. Doctors were sent to attend the major who was pronounced in perfectly good health and that his 'Intellectuals' were sound. They said he was suffering only from 'an exulcerated Conscience' which in their opinion could not be relieved until he was brought to justice.

The Lord Provost, still not wishing to believe the worst, felt that some ministers of the church should visit, inquire into his condition, then report. They did and reported that, 'The terrors of God which were upon his Soul urged him to confess and accuse himself.'

At this the Town Guard was dispatched to transport Major

Weir and the redoubtable Jean to the Tolbooth, the City Jail which dominated the High Street where Parliament Square is now. When the Guard, accompanied by two magistrates, proceeded to apprehend the villain, Jean urged the baillies to secure the major's staff since if he was allowed to grasp it, 'he could certainly drive them all out of doors, notwithstanding all the resistance they could make.' So the wizard's wand was duly impounded, along with sums of money wrapped in rags.

The stick was at all times kept away from the Tolbooth's most celebrated prisoner of the day. The universal belief existed that it had been given to the major by the devil at the end of the meeting in which Jean and her brother had sold their souls to the fiend while journeying to Musselburgh. Its diabolical powers were acknowledged by the major throughout his confession.

Their prisoners safely locked up, the baillies adjourned to a tavern in the West Bow. They still had with them the major's money which was put into a bag, which had held some pieces of cloth, and the rags were thrown into the fire. These, 'after an unusual manner, made a circling and dancing,' as they burned. Another rag containing 'a certain root' was also burned. It 'circled and sparkled like gunpowder, and passing from the Funnel of the Chimney, it gave a crack like a little Cannon, to the amazement of all that were present.' The money was taken home by one of the baillies and placed in a cupboard. The family, however, were unable to get to sleep 'for a terrible noise within the Study like the falling of a house.' They were removed by a servant to the house of the other baillie, where precisely the same thing happened.

Back in the Tolbooth, the major was visited endlessly by all the notables of the day. The Lord Bishop of Galloway and the Dean of Edinburgh both attended his cell. Always quite willing to horrify them with tales of his past, he remained adamant on his refusal to accept repentance.

It was actually sister Jean who was always more forthcoming about their dealings with Satan. She inherited her witchcraft from her mother, together with an unholy mark on her brow. The 'Devil's Mark' on Major Weir was to be found on his shoulder. It was Jean who admitted that she and her brother had made a compact with the devil 'and that on the 7th of September, 1648, they were both transported from Edinburgh to Musselburgh and back again in a Coach and six Horses, which seemed all of fire.' Also, 'she knew much of the enchanted Staff, for by it he was enabled to pray, to commit filthiness not to be named.'

On Saturday, 9 April 1670, the old couple were brought to trial in Edinburgh. The Lord Advocate prosecuted. No one defended. None dared. They were tried together on separate indictments: the major's crimes being more those of flesh and blood than of witchcraft and sorcery. Both admitted their guilt. Many witnesses were called to tantalise the court with descriptions of their misdeeds.

The jury found them guilty. Sentence of death was pronounced. Major Weir was to be taken on Monday 11th to the Gallow Lee at Greenside between Leith and Edinburgh and there, 'betwixt two and four hours in the afternoon' to be strangled at the stake till he was dead and his body to be burnt to ashes. Jean was to be hanged in the 'Grass Mercate of Edinburgh' on Tuesday 13th.

The major, being too old to walk from the Tolbooth to the Gallow Lee, was dragged on a sled, the horse being pulled by the hangman. On the spot of the burning, where Greenside Church was later built, it is recorded that the major's dying words when the rope was put around his neck, were, 'Let me alone, I have lived as a Beast and I must die as a Beast.' Also burned at the same time was his stick. Witnesses testify that both the major and the staff 'gave manifest tokens of their impurity'.

The major died with dignity. Not so his sister, Jean. When a minister went to the Tolbooth to inform her of her brother's demise she was apparently more interested in the fate of the staff. When told it too had been burned, 'she nimbly and in a furious rage fell on her knees, uttering words horrible to be remembered.' Thereafter she informed the minister that she intended to die 'with all the shame she could'.

Sadly, the minister took this to be an indication of her sorrow and regret. How wrong he was. The meaning and her intention were quite different. Lamont, the contemporary diarist, records, 'On the scaffold she cast away hir mantell, hir gown tayle, and was purposed to cast off all hir cloaths before all the multitude.'

The executioner was commanded to speed up the proceedings, presumably before Miss Weir caught a chill. Doubtless after further attempts at indecent behaviour designed to offend the assembled Presbyterian gathering, she went up in flames.

Were that the end of the story it is unlikely that the major and his sister would have gained such a notorious place in Scottish criminal history. Before we conclude we must dwell a little on the abode of the wizard in the West Bow. It survived its owner by two centuries, fully one of these being without a tenant. It soon became a place of dread and developed a mythical reputation of its own.

We learn of a 'gentlewoman' and her maid who were returning home from Castle Hill at midnight. As they passed by the house they saw 'three Women in windows, shouting, laughing and clapping their hands.' Unseemly but not supernatural. Worse was to come for just at Major Weir's door 'there arose as from the street a Woman above the length of two ordinary femells.'

'This long-legged spectre' writhed, laughed and followed the ladies in 'Stinking-Closs' (close) where the ghost filled the whole area with a blinding light as if she was surrounded by 'a great multitude of People' carrying flaming torches. The ladies ran for their lives.

As time passed and fact became myth and myth became legend, the 'Magical Staff' assumed even more marvellous proportions. It was said (with great authority) that it used to run errands for its master and would answer the door of his house to lead visitors to the major. Also, when the major went out at dead of night the stick would go before him in a full state of infernal illumination. On innumerable occasions locals returning to the Bow late at night after spending some boisterous hours in the howffs of the Lawnmarket were met by the wizard, mounted on a headless charger, bursting forth from the Stinking Close only to gallop furiously away 'in a whirlwind of flame'. During the early evenings of winter, decent folk returning home could see all the windows of his house ablaze with light, loud music accompanying the dancing of fearful shapes.

Most common and popular of all the sightings which so frequently disturbed the inhabitants of the West Bow happened 'in the chill unchancy hour before the dawn'. Thundering down the close came the clattering of hooves and the groaning and creaking of axles. This was the 'Muckle Deil himsel' driving his six coal-black horses which pulled his fiery coach. And where would the devil stop? Why, right at the major's house of course! Those who had not retreated back to their beds by this time would witness the damned face of the major passing through the panes of broken glass into the street.

One hundred and fifty years having passed since the death of Major Weir, an attempt was made to find a tenant for the house. One was found bold enough to occupy it. A Sergeant William Patullo agreed to share the house with the spirit of

Old houses, West Bow

the warlock. By around 1819 Patullo was little more than a drunken old reprobate and doubtless revelled in the speculation which spread round the city. Patullo and his wife moved in. On their first night the couple lay awake for some time. Just as the embers of their fire died out, 'they suddenly saw a form like that of a calf, which came forward to the bed, and setting its fore-feet upon the stock [bed-foot] looked steadfastly at the unfortunate pair.' Sergeant Patullo and his wife moved out the next day.

The house was demolished in 1878, since when Thomas Weir and Jean have returned to their childhood village in Lanarkshire where we have it on good authority the diabolical pair can still be seen.

DROPS OF BLOOD

On 1 June 1661 Revd Mr James Guthrie suffered death at the hands of the Common Hangman of Edinburgh. Several weeks after Guthrie's head had been fixed on the Netherbow Port, Lord Middletown, the King's Commissioner passed through the gate in his coach. Some drops of blood fell from the head upon the carriage. Try as he could the coachman could not wash off the blood. Physicians were consulted as to the possibility of the blood dripping so long after the head had been put up and on the impossibility of getting the blood stains out of the leather. But with all their combined knowledge and experience they could give Lord Middletown no satisfaction. The roof of the carriage had to be renewed.

THE MISSING GYPSY

Until the Anatomy Act of 1832, that aspect in the teaching of medicine at Edinburgh University was much hindered by a lack of bodies. A charter of 1505 allowed for one body annually to be used for dissection. Thus body snatching became a necessity.

The University of Edinburgh

Although no surgeon would openly admit to being involved in the practice, none could do without it. On 20 May 1711 the College of Surgeons protested against body snatching. On 24 January 1721 a clause was added to prevent apprentices from violating graves. The Edinburgh people did not take these pronouncements seriously nor believed that they were expected to take them seriously. Body snatching continued unabated.

One of the worst cases took place in February 1678. Four gypsies, a father and three sons were hanged together for killing another gypsy called Faa. To the city fathers of Edinburgh gypsies were nothing more than wild beasts of prey. The four were therefore speedily hanged, hastily cut down and buried together — their clothes still on (it was not thought worthwhile to strip them of their rags) — in a shallow hole in Greyfriars Churchyard.

Next morning the grave lay open and the body of the youngest, aged 16, was missing. It was remembered that he had been the last to be hanged, the first cut down and the last to be buried. Perhaps he had revived, thrown aside the covering of soil and fled. Others believed that the body had been removed by some surgeon and his servant for the anatomy class. The body, as with so many, was never found.

BLAME THE CHURCH

Comets in the late seventeenth century seemed to attract even more attention than they do today. During December 1680 a formidable comet was seen over Edinburgh on many occasions. It rose in the west from a small star which appeared a little after daylight was gone. It moved northwards and developed a 'prodigious long tail'.

What did it mean? To the people of Edinburgh 'comets are thought to portend war, devastation, blood, ruin, conversions of states, catastrophes of kingdoms, deaths of great men, sterilities, famines and plagues.' Whether these happened simultaneously or only one or two at a time we are not quite sure. But what was to be done? Quite simply ministers should be banished, confined to their homes or imprisoned, and so it was done.

THE WRONG PARTNER

Principal among the persecutors of Presbyterian Scotland was Sharp, the Archbishop of St Andrews, whom the reformed church referred to scathingly as 'Sharp, the Judas, the Apostate'. Years before his death he was believed to be in league with the devil. On one occasion he accused Janet Douglas in front of the Privy Council of sorcery and witchcraft and suggested that she should be packed off to the West Indies to work on the king's plantations.

Not enamoured by this idea Janet said, 'My Lord, who was

you with in your closet on Saturday night last between twelve and one o'clock?' The Privy Council now became quite animated and a general pricking up of ears took place in anticipation of discovering some small piece of scandal about the archbishop. Sharp ignored the question. Not to be deprived however the Duke of Rothes took the girl aside and promised pardon for information. Reluctantly, ever fearful of the consequences, she replied, 'My Lord, it was the muckle black Devil.' This was not the partner the Privy Council had hoped for.

THE SWEET SINGERS

At the time when the church was going through a particularly difficult period at the end of the seventeenth century, a strange religious sect grew in the city called the Sweet Singers. This

Edinburgh from the South

name derived from their frequent meeting together and singing those tearful psalms over the mournful state of the church. To many of those persecuted by the church it seemed incredible that heaven should not open itself and wreak havoc on the guilty. The little band of singers continued to sing while it became clear to them that the fate of Sodom and Gomorrah must fall on the wicked city of Edinburgh.

They decided they must flee and so we are told, 'they left their Houses, warm soft Beds, covered Tables, some of them their Husbands and Children weeping upon them to stay with them, some women taking their sucking children in their arms to Desert places to be free of all Snares and Sins and communion with others and mourn for their own sins . . . and there be safe from the Land's utter ruin and Desolation by Judgements.'

Where were these 'Desert' places to be found? In the Pentland Hills just to the south of the city. There they would sit and watch 'the smoke and utter ruin of the sinful bloody city of Edinburgh.'

Time passed, the heavens did not open and the city remained unconsumed. A troop of dragoons were sent to round them up. The men were put in the Canongate Tolbooth, the women in the House of Correction where they were 'soundly scourged'. These good thrashings brought them back to their senses and they were one by one sent back to their homes and families.

THE POWER OF THE SERMON

Dr Gilbert Rule was Principal of the University between 1690 and 1701. As well as being a great academic he was also a powerful preacher. In some ministerial wandering in the Highlands he had to spend a night in a solitary house somewhere in the wild Grampians. At midnight a ghost entered his house and despite Dr Rule's forceful rebukes could not be made to leave him alone. He walked out of the house but was followed by the ghost wherever he went. Eventually, when the doctor reached some particular spot, the ghost vanished. The doctor returned to bed with teeth chattering from both cold and fear.

The next morning the ground outside the house was found opened and the skeleton of a murdered man discovered. Gilbert preached on the following Sunday from the parish pulpit. His sermon on the judgement and wrath of God which would eventually befall all men was so powerful that an old man stood up and confessed to the murder. In due course the man was executed and the ghost walked no more.

LADY STAIR

One of the most fascinating qualities which, despite the Improvers, the Old Town still possesses is the variety of closes which run off the main thoroughfare that is the Royal Mile. Many of the closes have tragically been destroyed to make way for what was presumably seen at the time as improvements. Many, however, still remain — each one quite different from the next and all bursting with history. The entrance to Lady Stair's Close gives to the adventurer no clue as to what will be found about halfway along its extent, namely a fine old mansion dating from 1622. This is Lady Stair's House. Its name dates from the early eighteenth century when the house passed into the ownership of the first Lady Stair — wife of the celebrated commander and diplomat, John, Earl of Stair.

Our story concerns this lady before her marriage to Lord Stair. It is not ghostly, but remarkably intriguing. Lady Eleanor Campbell, as she was, was first married to James, Viscount Primrose, at what was even for those days a fairly early age. Lord Primrose was an unmannerly gentleman with a violent temper. Although Lady Eleanor had developed a reputation for handling most men because of her force of character and superior intellect, the cruelty of Lord Primrose was too much for her. The treatment of his wife was more becoming of a barbarian than a man of Scots culture and civilised behaviour. So much so that Lady Eleanor was convinced that one day she would be murdered.

One morning while she was dressing herself in her own chamber, near an open window, this fear almost became a reality. For standing behind her and indeed moving directly towards her came his lordship clutching a menacingly drawn sword. He had quietly opened the door and although his face was full of anger and hatred he still had sufficient control to approach her with stealth. Had she not caught his reflection in the glass he undoubtedly would have run her through with his naked weapon. Fortunately, we are told, she secured her escape by leaping out of the window into the street. Half-dressed, she sought refuge at the house of her mother-in-law where the whole story of the unhappy marriage was unfolded. It would appear that the senior Lady Primrose's sympathies did not lie with her son.

No reconciliation being in any way possible, the couple separated. Lord Primrose soon afterwards went abroad where doubtless he would come to no good. During his absence, a foreign fortune-teller came to Edinburgh. He seemed to be an entertainer of many talents, for as well as conjuring, he also claimed to be able to inform any person of the present condition of any other person, no matter how far away.

Like many others in the city, Lady Primrose decided to go to the lodgings of this wise man in the Canongate. She was accompanied by a female friend who was aware of the curiosity which Lady Primrose wished satisfied. Disguised in the plaids of their servants, the two ladies ventured forth at dead of night.

Lady Primrose described the man, her husband, about whose present location and condition she was keen to find out. The fortune-teller led her to a large mirror in which she saw not her own reflection, but a strange image. Not static like a painting or portrait, but a scene which resembled a company of players on a stage; positioned but movable. The set, as far as Lady Primrose was concerned, was a church. The scenario being enacted before her eyes was a wedding ceremony.

The preliminary service being concluded, the priest was about to join the bride and groom in wedlock. Just at the point when the couple were being invited by the priest to join hands, a new character appeared on this magical stage.

A gentleman, whose arrival seemed to have been long awaited by the rest of the group, entered the church. Hurriedly he made his way towards the bridal party. His face at first bore nothing but the countenance of a friend who was there by invitation but who had arrived late. Abruptly, this demeanour changed. The man stopped short; the look on his face became one of wrath, so much so that in front of the priest and the whole congregation he drew his sword. Brandishing it with great determination, he rushed up to the bridegroom who prepared to defend himself.

The scene became one of anger and confusion and of great anguish for the bride. Becoming cloudy and indistinct, the scene entirely vanished from the mirror and the eyes of Lady Primrose. What had this been? None of it had meant anything to the fortune-teller. But for Lady Primrose, the whole scene had been all too clear and identifiable; yet almost too fantastic for words.

When Lady Primrose arrived home in a state of something between shock and amazement, she set herself down to write a full and detailed account of all that had been seen. For preciseness she added the date to this tale. Before a witness she sealed the narrative and placed it securely in a drawer.

Some time after, Lady Primrose's brother returned to Edinburgh from his travels. She enquired of him in a general way if he had by chance happened to see or hear anything of her husband, Lord Primrose. Not wishing to directly tell a lie, he answered by saying that he wished he might never again hear the name of his detestable brother-in-law. Lady Stair, however, pressed her brother more closely for information. Eventually he confessed that while in the Low Countries he had encountered Lord Primrose under very strange circumstances.

Having spent some time in one of the Dutch cities — it was either Amsterdam or Rotterdam — he had become on good terms with a wealthy merchant. This gentleman had only one child — a daughter who was very beautiful and sole heiress to a vast fortune. One day the merchant announced to Lady Primrose's brother that his daughter was to be married — to a Scotsman! The marriage was to take place within a few days, and, as he was a countryman of the bridegroom, he was invited to the ceremony.

Delighted to accept this invitation from his new and good acquaintance, on the due day he set off for the church. Perhaps through his lack of knowledge of the city, or because of the great preparations of attire required for attendance at a wedding, he arrived too late for the beginning of the ceremony. Fortunately, he arrived in sufficient time to prevent a beautiful young girl becoming the victim of a bigamous wretch — for the bridegroom was none other than his brother-in-law, Lord Primrose!

We are told by this stage in the telling, her brother knew that Lady Primrose probably would be near to collapse. The brother, of course, was unaware of the real reason for this condition. Indeed, it is said that she almost did faint, but apparently recovered in time to move to the bureau where she extracted from the drawer the sealed account of her mysterious vision.

One tantalising question still had to be answered before the seal was broken and the account read. When, Lady Primrose enquired, did this aborted ceremony take place? The answer given, the brother broke open the packet, still unaware of its importance at this time.

What he read in Lady Primrose's own hand of what she saw in a mirror in a house in the Canongate of Edinburgh was precisely what he saw in a church in Holland on precisely the same date hundreds of miles away. Vision and reality had come together.

MARY KING'S CLOSE

Where now stands the City Chambers once stood Mary King's Close and two other closes in this the most densely populated part of the Old Town. The close was named after Mary King, probably the daughter of Alexander King, chief proprietor in the area and advocate; also, we are told, 'a malicious papist'.

Mary King's Close was always a grim-looking place, particularly after an outbreak of the bubonic plague which frequently

The Royal Exchange

rampaged through the city. After a particularly severe attack of the plague in the seventeenth century the Council finally closed Mary King's Close for good — or that was their intention. To the Edinburgh people Mary King's Close was left only to those connected with the powers of darkness — the spirits of the unclean of the plague.

Time passed and by 1685 there was much pressure on housing in the capital. People needed to live within the city wall and so petition was made to reopen Mary King's Close for occupation.

Mr Thomas Coltheart, a respectable law agent from Mussel-burgh, and his wife moved from a lower part of the town to a better house in Mary King's Close. Their maidservant had been warned by neighbours that it was haunted. This warning was apparently not heeded for soon after they moved in, the maid deserted the place and her job — leaving Mr and Mrs Coltheart to defy the devil and his minions.

147

One afternoon Mrs Coltheart seated herself by her husband's bed. He had lain down that Sunday afternoon being slightly indisposed. Engaged in reading the Bible to him while he rested, she was suddenly aware of something happening to the left of her eyes. She looked round and was appalled to see a decapitated head. Suspended in mid-air, this was the head of an old man with a grey beard. His eyes gazed intently at her. She screamed at the sight and lay in a state of insensitivity till friends returned from church.

Mr Coltheart on being told sought to reason her out of her credulity and the evening passed over without much trouble. Later that night the couple had not long gone to bed when Mr Coltheart himself spied the same phantom head by the light of the fire, gazing at him with ghostly eyes. He rose from his bed, lit a candle and took to prayer. Sadly this had little effect.

In about an hour the bodiless phantom was joined by that of a child similarly suspended in mid-air, followed by the naked arm of a child suspended downwards, which, in defiance of all abjurations and prayers, not only persisted in remaining but seemed bent on shaking hands with him.

Poor Mr Coltheart addressed the very friendly but unwelcome intruder, engaging to do his utmost to right any wrongs it had received if it would only begone — but all was in vain. The goblin believed that the new residents were the intruders. The spirits persisted in making themselves at home. After all they seemed to have been civil enough. Their intentions were not unfriendly. If only they were permitted to have the run of the house.

Time passed. Deeper into the night journeyed this strange assembled group until the naked arm was joined by a spiritual dog. It mounted a chair, turned its nose to its tail and went to sleep. A ghostly cat then entered the room, soon after being followed by other and stranger creatures until the whole floor swarmed with them so that 'the honest couple went to their knees again within the bed, their being no standing on the floor of the room. In their time of prayer their ears were startled with a deep dreadful and loud groan, as if a strong man was dying. At which time all the apparitions and visions vanished!'

No faint-hearted man, Thomas Coltheart stayed in the house

until he died 'without further molestation' we are told. But at the very moment he expired a gentleman whose law agent and intimate friend he was, being in a house in Tranent — 10 miles from Edinburgh — was awakened while in bed with his wife, by the nurse who was afraid that something like a cloud was moving about the room.

The gentleman got a sword to defend himself against the unwanted visitor. At that point the cloud gradually assumed the form of a man and 'at last the apparition looked him fully and perfectly in the face, and stood by him with a ghostly and pale countenance.' The spirit was recognised as Thomas Coltheart. The gentleman demanded of him if he were dead and what was his errand. The ghost held up his hand three times, shaking it towards him and vanished.

Immediately the gentleman dressed and rode at haste to Edinburgh to inquire about this strange occurrence at its source. Arriving at Mary King's Close he found Mrs Coltheart weeping bitterly for the death of her husband an hour before.

THE GHOST ROOM

Bruntsfield House — ancient, massive, sombre, with small windows, crow-stepped gables and high sloping roof — has frowned over the Burgh Muir for centuries. Among its great architectural qualities, Bruntsfield House had a 'mystery' chamber. Long known as the 'ghost room' it was discovered in 1820 when Sir George Warrender came into possession of the mansion.

Frederick Richard Lee, the painter and Academician whom Sir George brought from London to examine the house, suspected the existence of a secret room through finding more windows outside than he could account for rooms inside.

An old woman who had charge of the house at first denied any knowledge of an unknown apartment, but frightened by

Sir George's threats she finally revealed a narrow entrance to the room hidden by a piece of tapestry.

The door was forced, the room was found just as it had been left by some former occupant — the ashes still in the grate. The dimly lit room was strewn with neat branches. But that was not all. Amid these were found three skeletons, one in the middle of the room, another in front of the fireplace and the third crouching near the windows. Blood stains were found all over the floor and four rusty swords discovered scattered around the room pointed to a desperate encounter and the escape of one of the contestants.

It is said that a dreadful fight had taken place between the three sons of the Brands of Bruntsfield and a young gentleman called Maubray of Barnbougle. This latter gentleman, though small in stature, was a fearful antagonist to face with a sword. Thus the three skeletons belonged to the three unfortunate brothers whom he must have picked off one by one.

THE DEVIL'S MARK

We are much indebted to Sir George MacKenzie of Rosehaugh who was King's Advocate during the reigns of Charles II and his brother James VII for providing a definition of the 'Devil's mark'. We are told on good authority that the devil inflicts it 'by a nip in any part of the body'. Sir George adds with scrupulous accuracy so that no mistakes may be made that 'it is blue'.

Other witnesses of the time say that it is 'sometimes like the impression of a hare's foot, or the foot of a rat or a spider'. So now we know.

A WARNING FROM THE BED

A gentlewoman died in Edinburgh in 1693. Some hours after her death, the body was laid on a bed, fully dressed in 'dead-linnings' (funeral clothes). While in the room a considerable number of gentlewomen saw the corpse rise and sit up on the bed. The corpse called upon one of the women three times. This woman was sitting at the foot of the bed. To this person it said, 'For lying, backbiting and slandering of my neighbours, which the world thinks little of, I am, by the righteous judgement of God, condemned eternally to the flames of Hell.'

The body fell back and spoke no more.

THE GREEN LADY OF MORNINGSIDE

When one says or hears the word 'Morningside', one conjures up in one's mind images of class, wealth, respectability and genteel old ladies hopping on a No 41 bus for a jaunt into town to have morning coffee in Jenners or afternoon tea at the George. Morningside is that kind of place.

But in true Jekyll and Hyde (or Deacon Brodie) fashion it was not always so. For now we must think of darker characteristics — jealousy, hatred, revenge and death — if we are to understand the truth about the Green Lady of Morningside.

Near the Myreside end of Balcarres Street, which lies in the centre of the district between the local park and the suburban railway, there took place a story of violence and passion equal in horror to any in Edinburgh's dark and sinister past.

The year was 1712. The setting, a huge, rambling mansion which to this day still towers over the more recent bungalows of Craiglockhart on the one hand and the playing fields of Myreside on the other. The property was owned by Sir Thomas Elphinstone, a former Governor of Maryland. Returning from the colonies with his amassed wealth, he bought the mansion, repaired and furnished it to the highest of standards then looked around for someone to share it with. Sir Thomas had been a widower for some time and his only son, John, a captain in the army, was seldom a companion for his father.

We are told that Sir Thomas was greatly respected by all in

Morningside but not a man to be crossed because of his sudden and violent temper.

While visiting William, 12th Earl of Glencairn, Sir Thomas met the lovely but poor Betty Pittendale. He was besotted by her and asked the earl if he could court her. Despite their 40 years age difference the earl agreed. His attentions and obvious love for her were so great that the difference seemed a mere bagatelle. Betty, however, was not so enamoured. Events overtook her and in vain she begged for the wedding plans to be delayed. All the more so because there existed a young officer whom she had met at the Glencairns' house in London. The young officer was known at the time only by his regimental name of Captain Jack Courage, and Betty Pittendale had fallen in love.

But Jack was posted to Ireland and so Betty agreed to her parents' wishes and married Sir Thomas. The coronet's son could not attend his father's wedding. But four months later he returned home — as a colonel.

The old man was in a fever of impatience to introduce his son to his beautiful new step-mother. In honour of the occasion a grand dinner had been arranged. The Glencairns, the Pittendales, the Earl and Countess of Cassilis and the Earl and Countess of Findlater were all present.

Colonel Elphinstone arrived at the mansion late and was at once taken to his room by his father where they pledged each other in a glass of claret. At last it was time for the returning hero to meet the guests and of course Sir Thomas's wife. In front of the assembled company the colonel stepped forward to greet his new mother. Struck with horror she saw that the young man was none other than her 'Captain Jack Courage'. What was to happen now?

The reader's imagination will not be overtaxed to foretell ensuing events. Living under the same roof, large though it was, always near each other, the two young people fell more deeply in love. There was only one honourable thing to do. Young Elphinstone had to go away.

At their last meeting Colonel Elphinstone asked for a kiss — the first and last — and swore that it would remain on his lips forever. The first and last it was. For as Lady Elphinstone held up her face, there was a scream, a shout and a roar. Sir Thomas stood in the doorway in one of his most extreme rages — clutching a dagger. He plunged it directly into her heart.

Almost as violently as his father, the young colonel pleaded their innocence. The old man cringed, begged forgiveness and demanded that Jack run him through with his sword. Instead Jack picked up the body of the lovely young girl, still clad in her green evening dress, took it up to her room, followed by old Sir Thomas, and laid it in her bed.

Next morning, having looked everywhere in the house, Jack found his father still kneeling by the bedside, the upper part of his body across the bed, his arms tightly embracing the dead body. He too was dead.

With too many unhappy associations connected with the house, Jack rented it out to his friend Colonel Lamington and his family. The new household consisted of the colonel's wife, their 15-year old son, a daughter, a governess and a tutor.

All was well for the first couple of weeks of their tenancy. Then gossip amongst the servants began to spread to the effect that the governess had been seen walking towards the tutor's room around midnight. But the governess, Anna Burness, denied it all. Mrs Lamington believed her and agreed to keep the story secret from both her husband and the tutor, Mr Stewart.

Nevertheless, the following morning, Mr Stewart arrived at the breakfast table rather nervous and excited. On being pressed as to his state of mind, he explained that the night before, having partially undressed, the door of his room opened and a lady in a green dress came in. The tutor explained in what great distress the young lady was and how piteously she wrung her hands. She proceeded towards the bed, looked in, and seeing that there was no one there she threw herself onto it. In vain Stewart inquired as to what she wanted, but the woman would not reply. Five minutes later the figure vanished.

The tutor retired for the night. Yet every hour, he said, the lady in the green returned to the bed, looked down on it sorrowfully and left again.

Colonel Lamington flew into a rage, questioned everyone

in the household who might have played such a practical joke, but discovered nothing. Not satisfied, the colonel ordered that an extra bed be put up in the tutor's room and he prepared to spend the night there. Once again the lady in green appeared. She looked so real that the colonel spoke to her, asking her what she wanted. But again, she vanished.

One hour later, the door opened again, and the woman rushed in. She reached the middle of the floor, when a second figure, that of an old man came in after her.

'You have disgraced both yourself and me,' the colonel heard the ghost say, whereupon he stabbed the lady in green in the heart.

Again and again the horrific scene of death was enacted; not just on that night but on every night to come. The colonel finally wrote to Sir John Elphinstone to cancel the lease.

Sir John realised something had to be done. Returning from India he brought back with him a wise old mystic called Kalidosa who specialised in the supernatural. Arriving at the mansion Kalidosa made his preparations. He drew the signs of the zodiac, and began to chant a weird incantation. The air of the hall grew stiff and dense. Then the figures of Sir Thomas and Lady Elphinstone appeared.

'Why have you summoned us?' came the words from the ghosts in low and wavering tones.

'You, the dead, are disturbing the living. Why are you doing so?' asked Kalidosa. 'Has anything been done to anger you?'

'Yes,' said Lady Elphinstone. 'You have buried me beside my husband and his coffin in the vault is resting on mine. It has caused me unspeakable torment, because we shall never agree. Take me away and bury me elsewhere, if possible where I shall afterwards rest in death with the man I ought to have married, and all will be well.'

Sir Thomas was asked if he agreed. He did, and the spell was over.

When Sir John Elphinstone went to the vault later, the coffin of the Green Lady was lying on the floor, alone. The lid was broken across and open. He saw the lovely face of his young Betty, a little waxen in death, smiling, a placid look on her face.

He ordered that a new vault be made. The coffin was transferred. And, years later, the body of 'Captain Jack' was laid to rest beside her. The Green Lady appeared no more. Now she lies buried with the man she loved . . . although today nobody knows where exactly the graves are to be found.

THE HEIRS AND GRACES OF WITCHES

It appears that in the eighteenth century and probably before, a process of confiscation took place after the incineration of witches. Their possessions were not cast out into the street for the mob to pounce on any of the objects which had been associated with evil. Not a bit of it! Some of Edinburgh's most notable baillies saw to it that their own highly respectable order fell heir to the goods and chattels of their, not always poor, victims. How little it took to brand and convict a woman of witchcraft.

An act of parliament as late as 1770 decreed that, 'All women, virgin, maid or widow . . . that shall betray into matrimony his Majesty's subjects by means of scents, paints, cosmetics . . . artificial teeth, false hair, hoops or high-heeled shoes shall incur the penalty of the law, now enforced against witchcraft . . . and the marriage shall be null and void.'

MERRY ANDREW AND SPUNE

By virtue of their profession, the body snatchers were not a group who sought publicity. They therefore remain very shadowy characters in Edinburgh's history. One exception to this was a group led by Merrylees, or more often called Merry Andrew. He was a great favourite with the medical students. Leighton in his *Court of Bacus* describes him graphically: 'Of gigantic height, he was thin and gaunt, even to ridiculousness, with a long pale face, and the jaws of an ogre. His shabby clothes, no doubt made for some tall person of proportional girth, hung upon his sharp joints more as if they had been placed there to dry than to clothe and keep warm.'

His gait was springy and his face underwent contortions of the least pleasant kind. His ways and manners were peculiar but well known and accepted by the people. Those with whom he came in contact seized every opportunity of tormenting him, generally much to their own intense satisfaction and amusement.

Another, and one of Merry Andrew's colleagues, was a worthy whose proper name is unknown but who went by the soubriquet of 'Spune'. He was physically broken down and mentally feeble. Leighton describes him to his readers: 'You would have said he bore all the honours of the science to the advancement of which he contributed so much.'

However, scientific aspirations were only partially the motives which promoted their employment. But for 'Moudewart', properly called Mowatt, the pecuniary results weighed much more than any scientific considerations.

'Moudewart', the third member of the group, was a plasterer by trade but he took to the business of a resurrectionist simply because he could make more money a great deal more easily.

These men made many purchases in the lower parts of Edinburgh, for not a few drunken, shifty creatures were willing to sell the bodies of their deceased relatives for a small remuneration. It was not uncommon for an arrangement to be arrived at before the final separation of soul and body.

Apparently, one night Merrylees was seen by a medical student standing at a close end. The student suspected that the body snatcher was watching his prey. 'She's dead,' the student whispered in his ear, quickly leaving the scene to escape identification. A moment after, Merry Andrew shot down the wynd, opened the door, and pushed his lugubrious face into a house.

'It's a' owre I hear,' said he in a loud whisper. 'And when will we come for the body?'

'Whist, ye mongrel,' replied the old harridan, who acted as nurse, 'she's as lively as a cricket.'

The unfortunate invalid was terrified but unable to do anything to help herself. Merry Andrew slipped out, and went in search of the student who played such a scurvy trick on him, but was of course unsuccessful.

However, the old invalid's end no doubt hastened by what she had witnessed came about on the following night. Merrylees, who heard the news, arrived with 'Spune' and entered the dead room with a sackful of bark. To their astonishment the old witch of a nurse had scruples.

'A light has come down upon me frae heaven,' she said, 'an' I canna.'

'Light frae heaven!' said Merrylees indignantly. 'Will that shew the doctors how to cut a cancer out o' ye, ye auld fule? But we'll sune put out that light,' he whispered to his companion, 'awa, and bring in a half mutchkin.'

'Ay,' replied the Spune, as he got hold of a bottle, 'we are only obeying the will o' God. Man's infirmities shall verily be cured by the light o' his wisdom! I forget the text.' And the Spune, proud of his Biblical learning, went on his mission.

He was back in a few minutes: for where in Scotland is whisky not easily got? Then Merrylees, filling out a glass, handed it to the wavering witch.

'Tak ye that,' he said, 'and it will drive the deevil out o' ye,' and finding that she easily complied, he filled out another which went in the same direction with no less relish.

'And noo,' said he as he saw her scruples melting in the liquid fire, and took out the pound note, which he held between her face and the candle, 'look through it, ye auld devil and ye'll see some o' the real light o' heaven that will make your cat's een red.'

'But that's only ane,' said the now wavering merchant, 'and ye ken ye promised three.'

'And here they are,' replied he as he held before her the money to the amount of which she had only had experience in her dreams and which reduced her staggering reason to a vestige.

'Weel,' she said at length, 'ye may tak her.'

All things thus bade fair for the completion of the barter when the men and scarcely less the woman were startled by a knock at the door which, having been opened, to the dismay of the purchasers there entered a person, dressed in a loose great-coat, with a broad bonnet on his head, and a thick cravat round his throat, so broad as to conceal a part of his face.

'Mrs Wilson is dead?' asked the stranger as he approached the bed.

'Ay,' replied the woman, from whom even the whisky could not keep off a look of fear.

'I am her nephew,' continued the stranger, 'and I am come to pay the last duties of affection to one who was kind to me when I was a boy. Can I see her?'

'Aye,' said the woman, 'she's no screwed down yet.'

Merry Andrew and the Spune slipped out of the house, followed by the stranger, who pretended to give them chase.

The stranger, it came out afterwards, was the student who thought fit to play a practical joke on the two worthies. The dead woman was decently buried, but the nurse quietly put the three pounds in her pocket.

DRESSED FOR THE PART

In the course of some transactions in Blackfriar's Wynd, Merrylees had — so they thought — cheated his companions out of ten shillings, an offence never to be forgotten or forgiven.

A sister of Merrylees, with unfortunate timing, happened to die in Penicuik. It occurred to Merry Andrew's unfeeling heart that he might make a few pounds by raising her body immediately after the internment. He said nothing, but the 'Spune', noticing from his appearance that he had some important project in hand, made enquiries which made him, as he said, 'suspect that Merrylees's sister was dead at last.'

The 'Spune' told the 'Moudiewart' so, and they agreed to lift the body themselves, as by doing this they would not only profit to the extent of several pounds, but would also be revenged upon Merry Andrew for his unfair behaviour towards them.

A donkey and cart were procured, and the two companions set out that night for Penicuik with all the necessary utensils. Between midnight and one o'clock they were at work in the kirkyard. Hardly had they begun when they were alarmed by a noise near at hand, but, after listening a moment, they thought they were mistaken, and resumed.

At last they got the body above the ground. Then they heard a shout and behind a tombstone they saw a white robed figure with extended arms. They fled in terror and set out for Edinburgh in all haste. The apparition was none other than Merrylees, who having met the owner of the donkey and cart, and been told that his two colleagues were away with them to Penicuik, suspected their design and had thus frustrated them.

Waxing biblically again that man shall not live on the fruit of the earth, Merrylees shouldered the body of his sister and set out for the city. Before long he came near his foiled enemies, and raising another demonic howl he forced them to leave their cart behind, as they found their legs would carry them home faster than the quadruped they had borrowed. This was the crowning part of Merry Andrew's expedition, for he put his burden in the cart, and managed at last to convey it to the Surgeon's Square.

BODY FIGHTERS

In the hey-day of the body snatchers, two of the most enthusiastic groups of resurrectionists were the students of Dr Cullen and Dr Munro.

Sandy McNab, a well-known lame street-singer of Edinburgh, died in the Infirmary. Cullen and his students placed the body in a box in order to raise it to their rooms above by rope. Munro's students wanted the body for their anatomy class. After some searching they found it in the box where Cullen and his students had left it. Munro's group moved the body to a different part of the yard, intending to lift it over the wall. They were however sighted by Cullen's gang who attacked them fiercely. A great fight broke out from which Munro's gang emerged victorious and in possession of the body.

MISTAKEN IDENTITY

A constant fear of medical students and professors alike was that they would one day recognise someone on the anatomist's table. A tale is recorded of a student at the University of Edinburgh. He saw on the dissecting table what he believed

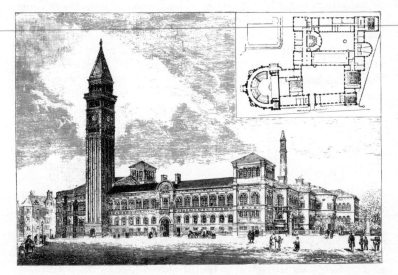

The Edinburgh University Medical School

Old West Kirk

to be the body of his mother. Half distracted he hurried home to Dumfries, and in the company of his father made a thorough investigation of the grave where his mother had been buried. He was however mistaken, for they found the body lying silently in its last resting place.

TO QUENCH A THIRST

We have known that for the price of a dram men have committed very dire deeds. One John Samuel, gardener, moved by an all too consuming thirst was arrested at the Potterrow Port as he tried to sell the dead body of a child. The child had been recognised as having been buried at Pentland the week before. Samuel was soundly whipped through the city and banished for seven years.

THE BODY IN THE SEDAN

The background to this intriguing story is unknown but this short extract allows the reader to realise that transporting exhumed bodies was no easy matter. It appears that one day in the bustling High Street of Edinburgh a dead body was discovered in a side street on its way to the Medical School and the dissecting room. The chairman and his assistant were banished from the city and the sedan chair was burned by the common hangman.

THE SNATCHERS SNATCHED

The ultimate crime of the body snatchers was to be caught. Everyone in Edinburgh knew of the work of the resurrectionists. It was an accepted way of enriching the teaching of medicine in the university, which was rapidly becoming the most advanced in the world. However, if a snatcher was caught he could expect no mercy.

On 9 March 1742, the body of a man, Alexander Baxter, who had been interred in the West Kirkyard of Edinburgh, was found in a house adjoining the shop of a surgeon named Martin Eccles.

Popular indignation had been raised by the suspicion, amounting almost to certainty, that the churchyards were being desecrated and it needed very little to cause a turmoil. The Portsburgh drum was seized and beat throughout the Cowgate. The populace demolished the contents of Eccles's shop, smashed the windows of other surgeons and it was with the greatest difficulty that the authorities were able to quell the riot. Eccles and some of his apprentices were brought before the court charged with the offence of being accessory to the lifting of bodies, but the charge was abandoned for want of proof.

Later, on the 18th of the same month, the house of a gardener named Peter Richardson of Inveresk was burned by the people on the suspicion that he had some hand in pilfering the village churchyard of its dead.

TWOPENNY BOTTLES

The Edinburgh correspondent of the *Newcastle Courant* writing on 28 July 1741 provides us with the following piece of absurdity:

'The people of Broughton, a small ancient village, near the city, are just now under a terrible pannick, by reason of a female ghost which they say publicly haunts the house of one George Bell, a blacksmith there, and vents her rage on the good woman of the house and twopenny bottles. This chimera draws a vast concourse of people to the house' — no doubt to see what fate befalls the twopenny bottles.

TENPENCE FOR A DRAM

In 1752, two women, Helen Torrence and Jean Waldie, were executed for the murder of a boy of eight or nine years of age. They would appear to have been nurses, and they promised some doctors' apprentices that they would supply them with a subject, proposing to do this by the abstraction of a body from a coffin, when they were sitting at the death-watch (for it was then the custom never to leave a corpse in a room alone).

They were either unsuccessful in accomplishing this, or were anxious speedily to redeem their promise and obtain their reward, for they took even more reprehensible means to obtain a body. They met the boy and his mother in the street and invited the woman into a neighbouring house to drink with them. She consented, and while she was sipping her liquor one of them went out to look for the boy. He was discovered leaning over a window. The woman carried him to her own house, where she suffocated him among the bed-clothes. The mother afterwards searched for her son, but could not find him. Meantime, Torrence and Waldie took the corpse to the surgeon's rooms, where they were offered two shillings for it, the one who had carried receiving an extra sixpence.

The ladies were displeased with the lowness of the price, but the students would only increase it by tenpence, which was given them for a 'dram'. The facts of the case at length came to light, and the women suffered on the scaffold for their barbarous crime. The students of course did not.

THE LADY IN BLACK

A Mrs Gordon who lived in an ancient house in Chessel's Court often heard the sound of heavy breathing on the outer side of her front door as if someone had paused to rest after climbing a steep stair. Over and over again she would look out but there was never anyone there. It did not, we are told, cause her great concern.

Her 'guidbrother', however, had more definite evidence of the ghostly visitor's presence and 'near lost his mind' as a result. Sleeping in the main room of the house, in a bed half in and half out of a richly carved recess, Mrs Gordon's brother-in-law retired for the night. Suddenly in the dark hours of the night he awoke. As his eyes grew accustomed to the darkness he saw a terrifying figure glide from the recess. The apparition was a tall woman clad from head to foot in black with a black veil over her head. Her wide shift was of antique style which 'near took up the whole room'. He fled the house after bundling on his clothes in an agony of fright. He never spent another night in the house.

It is said that the apparition was that of a gentlewoman who had hanged herself in the recess in those days when the house was in its prime.

SHIP AHOY

When the great Robert Liston was a student at the medical school in Edinburgh, he heard from a country surgeon of an interesting case where a post-mortem seemed desirable in the interests of science.

Liston and some other students dressed themselves up as sailors and headed for the spot by boat for it was on the

Firth of Forth. The country surgeon's apprentice met them as arranged and everything went off well. The pirates repaired for refreshment leaving their sack under a nearby hedge. In the hostelry they spent a jolly time carousing with the serving wench. Suddenly a loud cry of 'Ship Ahoy!' startled them. The girl said it was only her brother and before long a drunken sailor staggered in the door with the sack on his shoulders. Throwing it to the ground he said, 'Now, if that ain't something good, rot them chaps who stole it.'

He produced a knife. 'Let's see what it is,' he said as he ripped the sack open.

However, the sight of the contents caused much alarm. The girl screamed hysterically and fled out of the door; the sailor, now entirely sober, followed his sister. Liston grabbed the body. He and his fellow students made for the boat. Within minutes they were back in Edinburgh.

GETTING RID OF THE OPPOSITION

It was not always doctors who employed the professional body snatchers. Often they were made use of for purposes which had not even the excuse of a desire for the advancement of anatomical science.

Two young men from the north, George Duncan and Henry Ferguson, lodged together in the Potterrow of Edinburgh. It appeared they were both rivals for the affections of a Miss Wilson, residing in the area of Bruntsfield Links. Ferguson was preferred and Duncan hated him because of this.

At last, disease carried away the successful suitor and his body was interred in Buccleuch burial ground. Duncan's hatred went even further than death itself, for he employed a well-known snatcher, who rejoiced in the cognomen of 'Screw', on account of his cleverness at raising bodies. They went together to the cemetery for the purpose of conveying the corpse of Ferguson to the rooms occupied by Dr Munro.

When they arrived they found Miss Wilson prostrate with grief beside the grave. At last she arose and departed. Within

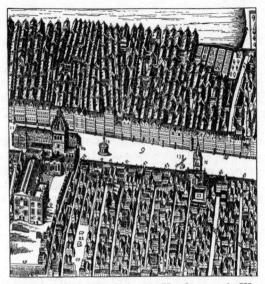

Edinburgh from St Giles to Hackerston's Wynd

minutes Screw had unscrewed the body from its intended last resting place, and was soon within the precincts of the college. The suitor who survived had the cruel satisfaction of knowing that the body of the other was on the anatomical table at the university.

THE GHOST OF BELL'S WYND

We wonder how many residents or visitors to the city who have passed by Bell's Wynd, between the Tron and St Giles, have realised that they were close to one of the most ghostly and sinister spots in the Old Town.

Just over 200 years ago George Gourlay, an Edinburgh locksmith and blacksmith, and his wife Christian lived in a second-floor house in Bell's Wynd. From the day they moved in George was fascinated, almost entranced, by the mysterious house below them. It had been empty and firmly shuttered for 21 years. This was far too long a time for any normal house in the Old Town to be unoccupied.

'Where had the owners gone? Why had it never been rented out? Why had it never been sold?' George asked himself. Christian should have been able to tell him something about the house. She had lived there before they were married, but she refused to talk about it.

In the many taverns of the High Street which he could visit after a hard day's work, George would hear stories of the house many years before; full of life one day, silent as the grave the next and forever more. The locals, many of whom had lived there all their lives, had their own ideas, but no one really knew. The more he heard about it the stronger the attraction of the house became. Eventually his curiosity proved to be too powerful and his training as a locksmith was too valuable a skill to ignore.

After a few drinks late one night in his local tavern, George went to investigate. Armed with a set of his locksmith's keys and a candle he went to the house below his own. He had no idea what he would see or find but his curiosity was going to be satisfied once and for all.

He entered easily and soon found himself in a long, narrow hallway, the smell of death and decay all around. It was ominously dark and the candle provided only enough light to see a few feet in front of him. His heart had been pounding from the moment he turned the key. He knew something sinister awaited him as he approached the four doors leading to rooms off the passage.

Going through the first door he came to the kitchen which showed many signs of being deserted in a hurry. On the table were plates and a sauceboat ready to be carried into the dining room. The skeleton of a goose was on a spit above the fireplace and the hearth was still full of cinders — it had never been cleaned out. Why had someone gone to so much trouble to prepare a meal which had never been eaten?

Furtively, he moved into the dining room and found the dining table set for a dinner for two. There was a knife behind a brick-hard loaf of bread and two full decanters stood near the wine glasses and plates. Who had this dinner been for? Why had it never been eaten? It was as if all had been spirited away without warning.

The locksmith's courage was beginning to wane as he slowly opened the bedroom door. He stood in horror — frozen to the spot! His bundle of keys crashed to the floor, the noise echoing round the room. As he stood there rigid, staring at a large four-poster bed with heavy velvet curtains drawn around it, a ghostly figure in white glided eerily and noiselessly from above the bed down towards him as he stood terrified in the doorway, passing by him, disappearing into the hallway, extinguishing the candle as it went.

Though he fumbled desperately to relight the candle he was determined not to give up, having come so far. He approached the bed. He took hold of the velvet curtains and pulled. In the bed, facing him — almost staring at him — was a skeleton, its white ivory teeth clenched tightly as if in agony.

Now George Gourlay had seen enough. In a state of frantic terror he raced out of the house and did not stop shaking until he reached the safety of his own bed. Christian was asleep, which was just as well. After what he had seen he didn't know if he would ever be able to speak again.

Next morning he was still in a state of shock. He had hardly slept. What had happened in the night was still fixed in his mind. But Christian knew that his state of mind and body could have been caused by only one thing. She would not discuss it. She didn't need to. She knew!

Two days later there was a knock at the door. Christian answered it and found an elderly stranger on the doorstep. Without introducing himself he began to ask the couple strange questions about the house below and enquired if George was a locksmith. Why had he appeared so near to the time when George had entered the house? Who was he? The old stranger asked if Gourlay would go down with him to the house below and help him to unlock the door. The locksmith refused.

'Then you know the secret?' asked the stranger, seeing the horrified look on his face.

'Aye!' he blurted out uncontrollably, 'I have seen the roasted duck an' the table set, and the decanters . . . an' . . . an' . . . an' . . . '

'Aye, the corpse,' said the stranger, hanging his head as he spoke.

At that point Christian suddenly recognised their visitor and fled out of the house screaming, 'It's the man himself! He's come back! It's the man! It's Mr Guthrie!'

She pleaded with a neighbour to fetch the fiscal and then poured out her story. The stranger, Mr Guthrie, had many years before been the last owner of the house. One night he had returned home unexpectedly and found his wife in the arms of another man. In a fiendish rage he had killed Mrs Guthrie's paramour and moments later, his wife. Christian had been their servant at the time. It was she who had been preparing the meal for Mrs Guthrie and her lover. Guthrie had paid her 10 guineas to keep quiet about the murders and preserve his good name.

The fiscal took an understanding, if not positively lenient view.

'Go, man, an' bury your wife. You have already paid a greater price, pursued round the world by your own conscience, than the law would ever have demanded.'

The ghost of Mrs Guthrie was finally laid to rest. Yet certain mysteries remain. How could Christian Gourlay live for 21 years directly above a house she knew contained a dead body? Why had Mr Guthrie returned for the first time only the very day after George Gourlay had been in the house and in fact seemed to know that the locksmith had been there? And what about the mysterious lover? What had Mr Guthrie done with the body?

We will never know.

THE SPIRIT OF BIBLE LAND

A middle-aged woman in an old fashioned tartan dress with a white mutch and apron was murdered on the landing of a top flat in Bible Land. We are well acquainted with her attire at the time of her death because she appeared so frequently in ghostly form at the scene of her murder. To the locals therefore her constant recurrences were not particularly frightening.

However her sudden appearance late one night so scared a young Mr Scrougal, who had been seeing his sweetheart home after a night's outing that he nearly fell downstairs in an effort to escape.

Some days later he summoned up enough courage to tell the girl's father what he had seen. Young Scrougal was highly offended when the father 'roared and laughed at him for taking so much notice of it.' Evidently the ghost appeared so frequently that no one bothered about it and Mr Scrougal was regarded as daft for making such a fuss over a solitary encounter.

The upshot was that the young suitor went into a proper huff, stopped courting the girl from Bible Land and married someone else shortly afterwards, presumably from a less spirited part of town.

THE FACE AT THE WINDOW

The wife of an Old Town butcher died after five years of marriage leaving her husband a widower with four young children. At a time when most men would be prostrate with grief, the callous butcher was having his evil way with a young woman in Provost's Close in company with a friend only four days after he buried his wife. While the two were deep in flirtation, the friend looked up and beheld at a window the clay, cold face of a dead woman — rendered more ghastly by her trailing grave clothes. Shrieks of horror attracted the attention of the amorous couple to this dreadful sight. The face seen at the window was identified as the recently deceased wife.

Believing this to be a rebuke to the new-found relationship, the widower desisted from further acts of passion — for a few days at least. But within a week the couple were at it again. Once more a similar apparition appeared to chill their ardour.

That night the widower fell into a sickness from which he never recovered. He soon followed his dead spouse to their new home in the grave.

THE GHOST OF THE HEADLESS WOMAN

Just over 200 years ago a General Robertson, who came from Lawers — the deserted village on the far side of Loch Tay — returned to Scotland from the wars in America. With him he brought his negro servant, Tom.

As his house at Lawers was being renovated, General Robertson and Tom stayed in an ancient mansion called Wrychtishousis which stood at the end of Gillespie Crescent, where the Royal Blind Asylum and shop now stand.

After only one night in the house, the general found his servant, 'Black Tom' as he was known, in a state of abject terror. Tom claimed that he had slept little that night, for he had been visited by ghosts. He claimed he saw a headless woman, carrying a baby in her arms, appear out of a cupboard, walk across the floor to the other side of the room, walk back, then disappear back into the cupboard.

Servant Tom pleaded with his master to allow him to sleep in another room. The general would have none of it. He warned Tom severely against the evils of drink and insisted that he should banish all absurd thoughts from his head.

Yet the next night the visitations continued. The ghost of the headless woman, dressed in white and carrying the child, appeared shortly after Tom had extinguished his light. Across the floor and back; across and back, slowly and silently, only to disappear once more into the thick heavy wooden built-in cupboard in this basement room.

Every night for three months the ghosts appeared. Eventually Tom gave up beseeching General Robertson to believe him. He grew thin and his health suffered greatly.

At the end of the three months, General Robertson's house

alterations at Lawers were complete. He and the demented servant finally left this fiendish house for good. General Robertson's niece moved into the Perthshire home as house-keeper and companion to the old soldier.

The incident was forgotten about until some years after the general's death when his niece received a visit from a friend. Wrychtishousis had become the home of this woman's family and knowing that her friend's uncle had once stayed there, she enquired if General Robertson had ever witnessed any strange occurrences.

The servant, who was still alive, was summoned and was only too glad at last to be given the chance to speak about the ghosts of the headless woman and the baby he had seen each night. Although the room was no longer used as a bedroom, the grim tale that was unfolded matched the suspicions and experiences of the new owners.

When Wrychtishousis was taken over by the Merchant

Wrychtishousis

Company and turned into a school and hospital with the money left by James Gillespie, many alterations had to be done to the house. As workmen were beginning the renovations in the basement, the built-in cupboard in one of the rooms was removed. The workmen noticed that the floorboards had been cut away and the boards replaced where the cupboard stood.

Suspicious of why this had been done, the workmen made a horrible discovery. Beneath the floor they found a coffin — damp and rotting. It contained the skeletons of a headless woman and a baby lying on top of her, inside a white pillowcase. Nearby the coffin were a thimble, a pair of scissors and a confession written by the murderer. But most gruesome of all was the fact that it was clear that the coffin was home-made — and made too small for the woman to lie in. So her head had been cut off to make the body fit!

The confession finally cleared up the whole macabre mystery. Many years before, the owner of Wrychtishousis had gone abroad to war. This wealthy young man left his wife and child in the care of his younger brother. Tragically, the soldier died and all his wealth passed to the baby boy. This was too much for the younger brother to take. So he killed his sister-in-law and her child, his nephew, in order to inherit the wealth and the house.

Do we wonder if servant Tom would have slept any more soundly if he had known the awful secret which lay beneath the wall cupboard? The next time you sleep in a room with a built-in cupboard in which to hang your clothes, take a few seconds to investigate it. You never know what was there before it was made, or what may still be buried underneath.

A GOOD ANGEL

Dr A. J. was sitting up late one night reading in his study, when he heard a footstep in the passage. Knowing the family were, or ought to have been, in bed, he rose from his chair. Looking out into the corridor he saw nobody and so returned to his study. Presently the sound recurred and he was sure there was somebody, though he could not see him. The footsteps, however, evidently ascended the stairs. He followed them till they led him to the nursery door. He opened it to check that no intruder was present and found that the furniture was ablaze. Thus, but for the kind offices of this good angel, his children would have been burnt in their beds.

SWORN TO SILENCE

At the end of the eighteenth century a beautiful young woman dressed in night attire appeared in the heart of a great fire which burned down a house in the Canongate. At the scene she was heard to cry, 'Once burned, twice burned, the third time I'll scare you all!'

It was said that she was a lady of good family. Beautiful and accomplished, she had lived in a fine house which formerly stood on the site of the fire.

One dark, windy night a minister was brought by sedan chair to a remote part of town, to give the last rites for the dying at that house and was astonished to find a healthy young woman who had just been delivered of a child. He had been taken to the place blindfolded and though he protested to those who had brought him that she was not dying, he was forced at pistol point to proceed with his office.

After performing his task, he left the house and only a few steps from the door he heard a shot. As he was transported home, a purse of gold was forced into his hand, and he received a warning that any reference to this event would cost him his life. The next day he was told by his servant that a great mansion house at the head of the Canongate had been burned down and that the daughter had died in the flames. After his departure from the house the minister had been so fiercely sworn to silence that he remained so. Only later did he confess to fellow ministers. Tradition lingered on that this was the reason why the ghost of the murdered woman made her threat.

SAVED BY THE SNATCHERS

The body of a wealthy woman was buried in Greyfriars Kirkyard one day around the beginning of the last century. The newly dug grave was duly visited by that educationally motivated band of men, the body snatchers. Excavating at speed, as they always did, their eyes were soon dazzled by the sight of a number of valuable rings on the woman's hand. A small saw was taken from their indispensable bag of tools. The act of severing the fingers began.

To their horror the 'dead' woman sat up in her coffin and let out shrieks of pain which echoed as far as Candlemaker Row. The sacrilegious pair took to their heels and fled.

It appears that the old woman had been buried in a trance, an occurrence said to be common at a time when doctors' certificates of death were not the essentials they are now.

The old woman survived.

Greyfriars Churchyard

FAMILY DREAMS

Mr R.E.S., an Edinburgh accountant, when 15 years old had left home in Dalkeith to stay with a friend in Prestonpans. He dreamt on the Sunday night that his mother was extremely ill. He woke, startled with the thought that he must return home immediately but, on reflection, decided against it. After all she had been fine when he left and it was only a dream. The dream however returned as he slept and he decided to take action, hurriedly dressing and rushing from Prestonpans.

On arrival at Dalkeith before daylight he learned that his mother had been seized with British cholera and was lying unconscious upstairs constantly crying, 'O Ralph, Ralph! What a grief you are away.' When he was admitted to her room, she was beyond recognising him. She died the next day.

The elder brother of Mr R.E.S. was assistant surgeon on board the *Gordon War-Brig* in 1810. Both men as youths remember being told of a dream their father had. He dreamt that his elder son would be promoted to the *Sparrow-Hawk* (a ship which no one had heard of). When the father related the dream to his family they laughed. There had been no correspondence with the son for several months.

A letter arrived the next week in which the son proudly told his family of his promotion to the *Sparrow-Hawk*.

MADEMOISELLE VERNELT

In a period of a few years just less than a century ago, George Street, the elegant main street of Edinburgh's New Town, was the haunting ground of one of the city's most enigmatic ghosts.

This spirit was no fearsome night-time apparition, but a young lady, tall and graceful, witnessed by those who had the powers, in broad daylight as if she were taking a leisurely afternoon stroll among the well-to-do Edinburgh citizens.

The first indication that all was not as it seemed was,

to one witness, the clothes she wore. Her coat had a high collar with blue velvet facing, sleeves which were full at the shoulders and a band of blue velvet drawn lightly at the waist. She wore a small hat with two large plumes placed high on the side. Other items of her attire were also considerably out-of-date.

By this stage only the witness's curiosity had been aroused. As he approached this young lady he was struck by her very pale yellow hair and her startlingly fair complexion. Overtaking her, a cold chill ran through his whole body. Her face was the face of the dead!

The strange proceedings continued as she progressed along George Street towards its junction with Dundas Street. No one else seemed to notice her. No one gave her clothing a second glance. But a number of passers-by uncontrollably shivered as they came close to her. As she prepared to cross the road an elderly gentleman, having finished his traverse, walked straight into and through the phantom young lady.

A few paces further on she paused and then glided into a chemist shop. Only a few steps behind, the witness followed, entered the apothecary's — and found that she was not there. She had disappeared. Inquiry was made as to her whereabouts, which was met with the same kind of abruptness that can still be found in some of Edinburgh's better-class shops today.

Some days passed before our witness returned to George Street. The day was one of those all too common occasions in Scotland when all the rain clouds of the world gathered together to deposit their load on the unsuspecting people of Edinburgh. It is not by chance that the mackintosh and the umbrella are the inventions of two of Caledonia's sons. Everyone's apparel on this day was the same — except for one young lady standing outside the Ladies' Tea Association Rooms. Dressed precisely as before, from her blue and white plumes to her high Louis heels, she was totally dry. Despite the deluge, not a drop touched her.

Our witness, anxious to get another, closer look, quickened his pace. As he darted past her he stared full into her countenance. The shock, the ghastly horror of her grim white face sent him reeling and staggering into the street. Willing himself not to faint, his gaze caught her form as it passed by a horse-drawn cab. As she glided by, the animal reared and shied and uttered noises that ascended from pain to abject fear and terror. Once again crossing the top of Dundas Street, she reached the chemist and entered therein.

Who was this lady? Why did she haunt one of Edinburgh's most unlikely thoroughfares for para-physiological experiences? Why did she always go into the chemist's? What had been her connection with this shop?

Answers to some of these questions were eventually forthcoming. Eighteen years before her reappearance in George Street (around the time when the spirit's clothes would have been in fashion), the chemist's shop was owned by a dressmaker named Miss Bosworth. This lady had retired to Bournemouth and it was she who was able to provide much of the information for our tale.

In 1892, an advert appeared in one of the daily papers. It had been placed by a Miss Jane Vernelt. Mademoiselle Vernelt, as she called herself, ran a costumier's business in George Street. The business was for sale — and at quite a substantial sum. Although initially put off by the figure, Miss Bosworth, who was interested in buying the shop, examined the books and realised that the business was prosperous, improving annually and patronised by a duchess and a number of Edinburgh's society leaders. The two ladies agreed on terms. Within a week Miss Bosworth was the owner.

All went well until a month after the transaction. Miss Vernelt returned to the shop. She appeared agitated and distressed. She screamed at Miss Bosworth. 'It's all a mistake! I didn't want to sell it. I can't do anything with my capital. Let me buy it back.'

Miss Bosworth tried to explain as politely and sympathetically as she could that this would not be possible. At this point Jane Vernelt began to behave as if she were totally mad. She shouted and screamed, seeming to have lost all her reason. So great was the disturbance that Miss Bosworth had to summon her assistant to forcibly evict Mademoisell Vernelt. No lesson was to be learned, however. Every day fi six weeks she returned, each time seemingly more derange than the last. Finally, Miss Bosworth was obliged to take legal action.

It was at this point that she discovered that Jane Vernelt was deranged. She had been suffering from a softening of the brain for many months. It was on strong medical advice that she had been told to give up the business and to place herself and her capital in the hands of trustworthy friends and relations. However, she delayed too long. By the time she did sell up, the resultant change, the disruption and her preoccupation with the fantasy that she was penniless all combined to accelerate the disease. This delusion of ruination grew more and more pronounced. Consequently, her actions became increasingly disturbed.

What was so particularly curious was that Miss Bosworth found that she too was one of that rare group of people who could claim to have psychic powers and could witness supernatural manifestations invisible to so many others. So

George Street

179

it was that some time before Miss Vernelt died, but long after she was put under permanent restraint, that she too saw the apparition gliding along George Street and in and out of the shop.

The spirit of Jane Vernelt was inexorably drawn to the last place of normality the body had ever known. Indeed, the death of the young lady some weeks later seemed to cause no interruption to the frequent visits.

Although there have been no reported sightings of Jane in recent years, no one can be sure if the distracted figure is laid to rest. Few, of course, would ever have the power to see her at all. But the next time you walk along the section of George Street between St Andrew Square and Dundas Street and you feel a shiver running down your back — look around. It could be Jane.

THE GHOST OF LIBERTON HOUSE

It is all too infrequently that we have evidence surviving to the present day for many of our tales. One exception to this is the photograph of the Ghost of Liberton House. Liberton, deriving its name from the leper colony which once was to be found in that part of the city outskirts, has a rich history of its own. Liberton House, like any self-respecting mansion, had its ghost, but in the years after the Great War its reappearance on one occasion was most unexpected.

The Marquess of Bute, the occupant of Liberton House at the time, arranged to have a photograph taken of a fine stone-framed doorway, over which was a similarly framed recess or window. An ancient chair stood on the right of the doorway and in the corner leaned an equally ancient sword.

When the photograph which was taken by a professional was developed, there appeared on the wall, high up on the left, near the recess, 'a large and extraordinarily sinister human face,

Liberton

with handsome features, and a smile as enigmatic as that of the Mona Lisa.'

Apparently the noble lord was an expert in all things psychical. To him the Liberton ghost photograph was one of the most weird and terrifying he had ever seen. The ghost continued to haunt the building but was never seen again in quite the same pose.

THE STEWARD OF THE DUKE

Exactly a century ago Robert Eliot Westwood, an instructor in the Royal Engineers, was stationed in Edinburgh Castle. He and his close friend, Tom, were lodged in the Governor's House, one of the most ancient and formidable parts of the

181

stronghold. Tom was an Englishman and a schoolmaster, two qualifications which prevented any profound belief in things supernatural. Although Robert had never actually experienced any spectral visitations first-hand he was not such a sceptic as Tom.

Conversations amongst the soldiers, especially at night, often returned to the topic of spirits — particularly if some of the other, more uniquely Scottish kind had been consumed. One night Tom and Robert found themselves discussing this most dangerous of all subjects as they locked up and prepared to ascend the dismal staircase to their bedroom on the second floor. The deeper the conversation, the more adamant Tom became that ghosts quite simply did not exist — never had, never would. Despite this it was Tom who went around locking every door possible, even to the point of using some of the solid medieval drawbars. Remembering some out-of-date superstition relating to such activity, Robert warned, 'One day you'll be burned in your bed. Be sure you put the candle out so that a tragedy like that does not happen to us.' Tom blew out the candle and got into bed. Before long they were both asleep.

A noise like the crack of doom brought them both up from the depths of sleep in a sudden terror. Although the door was securely bolted, the noise had unmistakably been of the front door being flung open. Both men listened. There were steps on the stairs. Heavy steps with a metallic ring, coming nearer and nearer. Tom gripped Robert's hand till his nails dug into the flesh. The door burst open, a blast of cold air came swirling in. The noise of the footsteps came rushing towards them. The whole atmosphere was filled with evil. A crack — then nothing more! A sudden ray of moonlight lit up the room. There was nothing there, except the open door.

Believing that if the bedroom door was open, the heavily bolted front door might be similarly so, the two soldiers went to check. It was, yet the bolts were still shot, but no damage had been done to the posts. Fearful of what satanic power had done this, the heavy old door was once more firmly slammed and the massive bolts put into place. Finally the great key was turned in the ancient lock. The men returned to their bedroom, locked the door, checked and rechecked that it was secure, then climbed into bed.

Eventually they both fell into a troubled sleep, but not for long. They woke with one yell of horror as the same noises as before struck their ears. The front door was flung open with a rending crash. The same iron steps on the stairs approached as before. Once more the room door was flung open, once more the sickening sense of evil and the uncanny blast of cold air. Whether or not anything visible had entered the room, the two terror-stricken young men could not say, for the moon had set and the room was dark.

With trembling fingers Robert lit a candle. The room was empty and peaceful. Only the open door showed that something unusual had happened. They knew the front door was open too. It took a great deal of courage to go down and shut it. Then once more within locked doors they lay awake, each uncomfortably remembering that in fairy stories strange things always happen thrice.

But they were not troubled again, and as it grew light they dozed off easily. Within what seemed only minutes later a more joyous knocking was heard at the door. This time it was one of their comrades who came to inform them that it was time to rise. Foolishly, but innocently, he inquired if the two men had slept well. Both gave the visiting soldier an earful, description of which would be too colourful for the reader to be presented with, but can be imagined.

It transpired that there was a rational, if supernatural explanation for the nocturnal events, which the soldiers were given at breakfast that morning.

The night of their stay in that room of the Governor's house was the anniversary of an incident which took place in 1689. In that year the Duke of Gordon was Governor of Edinburgh Castle. Expecting a siege, the Duke sent his wife and children over to Fife for safety. He sent them in the charge of his steward. Crossing the Firth of Forth a storm rose up, the ship sank and all on board were lost except the steward. He returned to the castle to tell his lord and the duke killed him on the spot in a room on the second floor — the very room where the two soldiers had slept.

Ironically, Robert Eliot Westwood was obliged to stay in that room many years later when he was married, but the ghost never troubled him again.

SO DREADFUL A MEMORY

An Edinburgh family with two daughters were on holiday in the country in an old-fashioned house with an unknown history. As the girls lay in bed one morning, the elder who was already awake beheld a dreadful figure. Its distorted form dancing in the sunlight distressed her so much that, unable to scream, she fainted. She resolved to tell no one of the apparition.

One year later at their home in Edinburgh the same daughter was doing her homework. Her younger sister was practising the piano, which annoyed the other. When asked to stop she refused and continued playing. After repeated requests the older sister shouted:

'If you don't stop playing, I'll show you something very horrible — something more horrible than you've ever seen in all your life.'

The sister continued to practise. The older sister then drew as accurately as possible the apparition from the country house. When the younger girl saw it she became terrified and stopped playing.

'Oh! did you see it too?' she exclaimed. 'Did you see it in the bedroom of the old house at . . . '

It transpired that both sisters had seen the monstrous spirit at different times and had separately resolved to tell no one because the memory was so dreadful.

LAST SIGHTINGS

During the last century, Mr C, a staid citizen of Edinburgh, was one day gently riding up Corstorphine Hill. Nearing the top he observed an intimate friend on horseback, immediately behind him. He slackened his pace to give him an opportunity to catch up. Finding that he did not come up as quickly as he should, he looked round again. He was astonished that no longer could he see him. The gentleman was particularly surprised as there were no side roads into which he could have disappeared. He returned home perplexed at the odd circumstances. On entering his house the first thing he learned was that during his absence his friend had been killed by his horse falling at Candlemaker Row.

A gentleman living in Edinburgh, whilst sitting with his wife suddenly arose from his seat and stepped forward with his hands extended, as if about to welcome a visitor. On his wife's inquiring what he was about he answered that he had seen so-and-so enter the room. She had seen no one. A day or two afterwards the post brought a letter announcing the death of the person seen.

Edinburgh from 'Rest and be Thankful' Corstorphine Hill

Mr H, an eminent artist, was walking arm in arm with a friend in Edinburgh when he suddenly left him saying, 'Oh, there's my brother!' He had seen him with the most entire distinctiveness, but on crossing the road was confounded by losing sight of him without being able to ascertain whither he had vanished. News came the next day that at that precise period of sighting his brother had died.

Similarly, two young ladies staying at Queensferry rose one morning to bathe. As they descended the stairs the sisters simultaneously exclaimed, 'There's uncle!' They had seen him standing by the clock. It was at that very moment he died in his house in Edinburgh.

IS ANYONE THERE?

A house in St James Street had stood empty for some time due to a variety of annoyances to which the inhabitants were subjected. One room in particular seemed to be the constant cause of distress.

A youth returning from a period abroad in the armed services was given this room to sleep in, on his arrival in Edinburgh. He knew nothing of the house. It was hoped by the owners that there would be no disturbance. In the morning, however, he complained of people looking at him between the curtains of his bed. The inquisitive starings went on all night. He refused to remain in the room or the house for another day.

The house then stood empty for a period until it was sold. A new owner was found and workmen began repair work. During the workmen's dinner break the Master Tradesman went to inspect progress. After an inspection of the lower rooms, he was ascending the stairs when he heard someone behind him. He looked back but saw no one, so continued — only to hear the same, but on further inspection, still saw nothing.

Feeling somewhat puzzled, he entered the drawing-room where, oddly, a fire was burning in the hearth. Wishing to dispel this strange sensation he resolved to sit by the fire for a while. He pulled a chair somewhat vigorously towards him. To his astonishment the exact sounds he had made were repeated as if an invisible person had pulled an invisible chair in the same vigorous manner and was sitting next to him.

The builder fled from the house.

No 17

A hundred years ago there lived a character in the vicinity of the Royal Botanic Gardens. Many strange stories of this man were passed around by the gossips of the area. There must have been something odd about him; handsome and well built, living alone in a ten-roomed house with never a caller at the door. Only twice a week did a charwoman bring him his provisions and attend to all his needs.

After he died, and the coffin removed to an unknown destination by an unknown firm of undertakers, the aged charwoman was seen to snib all the windows and to lock and double lock both the front and the back doors. For years the house remained thus — empty and neglected.

Years passed and stories began to circulate. The house at No 17 was no longer empty! No occupants were ever seen but noises were heard by the respectable inhabitants of No 16 and No 18. Around midnight the sound of voices would be heard coming through the walls. Voices of young ladies and the deeper tones of males. Yet no one was ever seen, nor any light shone through a window.

For a time there was much talk of the house being haunted, but nothing further happened, and for a generation at least the ghostly incident was forgotten. New residents moved into No 16 and No 18 but throughout all this time No 17 stood empty and desolate. That is until the early years of the Great War. The house then became a scene of great activity. Regiments of slaters, masons, plumbers, painters and joiners restored the house to its former glory. No one knew who sold the house but it was soon widely known that an English couple had bought it and that they intended to run it as a boarding house.

As a boarding house all seemed to be going well till first one, then a second, mysterious incident took place. The first was when a chambermaid heard voices coming from one of the attic bedrooms. Knocking at the door, she entered the room to draw the curtains and to turn down the bed, but found that no one was in the room.

The second incident was almost identical. Another chambermaid heard voices coming from the same room, and on entering found it unoccupied, but declared that she 'felt that there was someone standing beside her in the room.'

The proprietor decided to leave the room unlet for the time being. Unfortunately some students at the university got to hear about it and showed a rather morbid interest. By midwinter the proprietor was forced to let the mysterious room to a young married couple, as all the other rooms were occupied. Of course they were told nothing of the voices, but of course they heard them. Believing that the room must have been wrongly allocated they rang the bell on the landing to summon someone to put matters to rights. It was an elderly woman, Mary Brewster, who came in response to the bell.

Almost as soon as she entered the room she shrieked in terror. The housekeeper came bounding up the stairs, not stopping to say anything to the young couple. Entering the attic the housekeeper saw Mary Brewster rigid, clutching the brass rail of the bed, gazing upwards. Her expression was that of a person who had lost all reason. She had — and was never known to speak again. No other soul knew what or whom she had seen.

In Edinburgh, news travels fast and soon this incident came to the ears of the students. They approached the boarding house owner and asked if they could lay the ghost.

Among the students was one who was studying Divinity and who treated the matter with great seriousness. A thoughtful and popular young man, he and the boarding house owner agreed to a plan of action.

The student, Andrew Muir, was to obtain two hand bells that

were able to give clear penetrating and resounding peels. At 10 p.m. he and his bells were to enter the 'unfriendly room' (as it was now called). In the room directly below the owner was to wait. If Andrew Muir saw anything unusual he was to give a short, sharp ring on the smaller, higher-toned bell. If he was in serious danger and wished assistance he was to ring the bigger, deeper-toned bell. This was the plan.

At the appointed time the two men parted. For a matter of ten minutes there was no noise. Suddenly the sound of the higher toned bell rang out. Then immediately after boomed the deeper tone of the larger bell. The owner raced up the stairs and flung open the door of the attic.

By the dim light of the paraffin table lamp a grim sight met his gaze. Slumped in the chair was the powerful figure of Andrew Muir and on his face what could only be described as a look of dread and horror. The young student had been frightened to death — and with added horror the second bell was heard to sound once more as it fell to the floor from the dead man's hand.

What Andrew Muir and Mary Brewster saw has never been known. The ill-fated boarding house at No 17 ceased to exist. A changed man, the owner retired. Again the doors and shutters were closed and never again was the house occupied. Today nothing remains of No 17, the whole street having been demolished, taking with it any chance of resolving this most sinister mystery.